The Cricket Who Wouldn't Sleep

Butter Flies

Runaway Smudge

Special thanks to all who supported this project
in one way or another and helped make it happen—
you know who you are!

Acknowledgements

Illustrations for
The Cricket Who Wouldn't Sleep
Ashley Lore

Professional photographs* for
Butter Flies, Runaway Smudge
Mike Biden
www.IFLYPHOTOS.COM

Photographs* for
Butter Flies, Runaway Smudge
Tom W. Hall
Els Wely
Lyn D. McMullen
C

Production, layout, cover design
Kathy Pearsall

Layout
Rowena Santo

Technical editing
Constance Smith

Creative editing
Arthur G. Gregoris

* Photos have been marked with photographers' initials.

Illustrations and photographs used with permission.

Thank you to Jyvanie Dow for lending Giveny her name.

A heartfelt thank you to the illustrator of the Woe Bee Gone bees, who prefers to remain anonymous.

Published by Write Dimensions
British Columbia, Canada
Copyright © 2006 The Cricket Who Wouldn't Sleep by: C
Copyright © 2006 Butter Flies by: C
Copyright © 2007 Runaway Smudge by: C

ISBN 978-0-9809992-0-4

Printed in Canada by Friesens Corporation

Published in British Columbia, Canada October 23, 2008

The Cricket Who Wouldn't Sleep . . . . .Page 5
(For ages 3 to 103)

Butter Flies . . . . .Page 17
(For ages 5 to 105)

Runaway Smudge . . . . .Page 37
(For ages 7 to 107)

The Cricket Who Wouldn't Sleep

Illustrations by Ashley Lore

G iveny was a young field cricket who lived in the tall grass that grew soft and green in the springtime, and then turned golden yellow in the hot summer sun.

He thought himself very happy, but Giveny had one small problem. You see, he couldn't close one eye without opening the other to make sure nothing in the world about him was missed.

He loved nothing more than to sing all night with the other crickets, but when the sun rose in the morning, he would just keep right on singing instead of closing his eyes and going to sleep like his father and mother and sisters and brothers. He would roam about from place to place, exploring new spots, finding new treasures and singing all the while.

When his father would say, "Giveny go to sleep now," the little cricket would reply, "I can't!"

His father would shake his glossy black head and say, "What you really mean is, you won't. The day may come when you will find yourself in trouble because you haven't listened to me."

Giveny felt sad then because he didn't mean to hurt his father by disobeying him, but so loved to sing and chirp and hop about that he couldn't see any harm in what he was doing. It didn't hurt the other crickets after all, and he knew his father would still love him. And, of course, his father did; however, it made his father sad to think that Giveny might fall into danger by going beyond the safety of his voice and not be able to find his way home again.

Giveny wasn't worried. He went his merry way, singing all night and exploring all day, chirping here, chirping there and feeling happy because he could do whatever he wanted and never close his eyes to sleep.

One day Giveny came upon a beautiful object the likes of which he'd never seen before. It was a large thing of pink and yellow on the outside with a dark opening that led to a jumble of interesting tunnels to explore. Giveny played and sang as he marched up and down the tunnels, feeling like he had found a wonderful new cave all his own.

After awhile he stopped to lean against a wall and rest his antennae, but the little cricket hadn't slept for several days and all that marching and singing had begun to tire him out. Soon he found that he couldn't keep even one eye open, no matter how hard he tried, and finally, Giveny fell fast asleep.

He dreamed of sailing through the air and entering a strange, new world where bright lights and loud noises brought him abruptly awake. He leapt up, bumping his head against the tunnel roof.

"I must escape from this place," he thought, starting to worry.

He climbed back out, noticing how steep the way had become, and saw that his tunnel had moved. It was no longer where he had found it by the tall grasses of his home.

Gone were the towering trees, the gentle breezes and the warm sun. Giveny couldn't even see the sky.

"Father, help me!" he sang out, jumping free of the tunnel, which was really just a gardening glove that had been left sitting outside.

His father's voice did not come back to him and Giveny was truly frightened for the first time in his life. He didn't know what to do. The lights were so bright and there was so much noise.

It was only a basement where the gardening tools were kept, but the little cricket didn't know that. He jumped about, crying for his father and trying to find his way out of this scary dream.

Then things got worse. He could hear loud screams and a voice said:

"Look! A big, black spider on the ceiling! Kill it!" and suddenly a dark object in the shape of a shoe came flying at the little cricket, just missing his poor head.

"Aw sis, you're such a scared-y-cat, it's just a cricket," another voice answered. "I'll get it."

And another object, in the shape of a fly swatter, whacked against Giveny's back legs as he jumped again for his very life.

"Father, father, help me!" he sang as loud as he could in a great panic.

Giveny knew now that his father had been right. He was afraid that he was so far away from his father's voice that he was beyond any help. He jumped and jumped and jumped again, crying as only a very frightened cricket can do.

"What are you kids doing down there?" an older voice suddenly asked.

"We're trying to kill a cricket, Daddy," came the reply from the two younger voices.

Loud footsteps approached and then the older voice was heard again.

"Wait. Don't kill it. Listen."

Giveny heard a harsh, grating noise and jumped again, waiting for something to smash into him, but now another sound met his ears. It was the soft, chirping voices of his family—his brothers and sisters! Cool evening air washed over him and he knew he should make his way toward it but he was so petrified with fear that he found he couldn't move.

The older voice spoke again.

"You see children, it's his father calling to him from the fields, and he so wants this little cricket to come home where he'll be safe. Let's help him get there."

Giveny listened with sudden joy as he realized that the older voice had spoken truly. Now that he was really quiet, and had stopped all his singing, chirping and hopping about, he could hear the dear sound of his father's voice calling him to come back from wherever he had strayed.

The little cricket had a moment of fear when two large hands surrounded him, but they didn't squash him for being where he shouldn't have been. Instead, they carefully carried him to the open window and gently set him down on the ledge.

Giveny looked up and smiled at the warm hands, not knowing how else to thank the one who had helped him. Then he turned and made the biggest leap he had ever made in his life, landing right next to where his father sat singing his sorrow at losing his son.

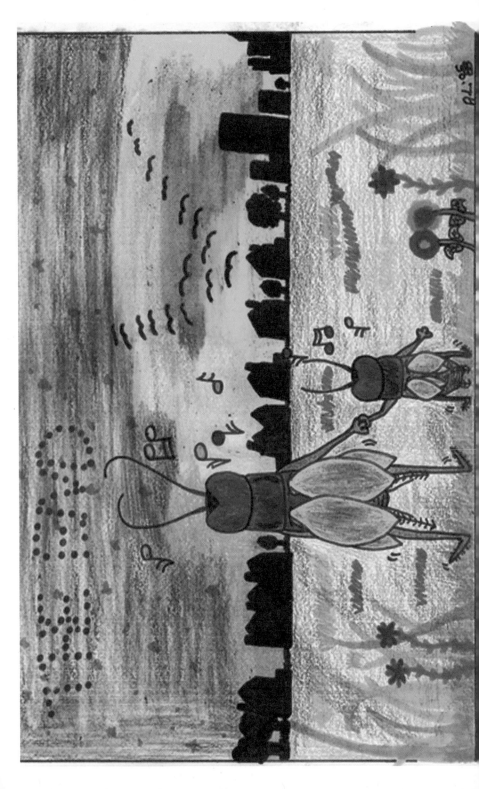

What joy they both felt! All the other crickets gathered around to welcome him home and sang extra loud that night to thank the warm hands that Giveny told them had helped him back to his father when he was so lost and alone and afraid.

"Can you sleep now?" his father asked him.

"Yes. I guess I always could," Giveny admitted, feeling ashamed. "Father, when I was in that dark tunnel I dreamed that I was flying. I knew then that I really just wanted to have all my feet on the ground, and sleep at the right time, so that I could sing my very best for you when I was awake."

The father cricket smiled at the wisdom his son had gained and together they began to sing a new song.

Butter Flies

EW

MB

MB

The garden was a lovely place with trees and hedges surrounding a multitude of bushes and plants loaded with the rich bounty of the earth. Butterflies abounded throughout the flower-filled garden of reds, yellows, blues, oranges, whites and, of course, purple. Other creatures lived there too: some with wings of gossamer, some with wings meant for flying fast without the worry of looking pretty, and still others who had no wings at all.

There were crawling things and fuzzy worms, hard-backed beetles and stinging wasps, long-legged spiders, spittlebugs and bumbling bees.

The flower of one particular bush in that garden seemed to attract many of these crawling, climbing, fluttering, flying things. At first glance, the Butterfly Bush seemed rather plain. It was not tall and powerful like the sunflower, nor brilliant like the daffodils, nor stately like the roses, nor as fragrant as the lilacs; however, the nectar was sweetest from its purple flower that bowed its head in humbleness against the strong, sturdy stems that gave it birth and surrounded it with an abundance of rich green leaves.

It was only natural that the butterflies chose to think of it as their bush, since it was named for them after all. A few of the more beautiful butterflies did not like to see the crawling, climbing, flying things come around it and drink its nectar. Some even thought their cousins, the plain brown or gangly grey moths, really had no business being so close to their bush.

Amongst the butterflies there was one especially handsome creature with wings the colour of spun gold that seemed to shine in the light of the sun. His name was Bellisimo and he knew how beautiful he looked to others and thought he had a right to be proud.

Bellisimo's large, multi-coloured family was a sight to behold as they flew about the Butterfly Bush, yet there was one sister who was not quite as fine looking as the rest—even her name was plain. Butter they called her though her wings were not yellow, but brown and white with a small bit of blue. Butter often felt her plainness, noting that instead of a slender body like the other butterflies she had a middle that was big and wings not quite as broad as they could be.

She would go to the Butterfly Bush and ask it why she hadn't been made as beautiful as her splendidly coloured sisters and brothers.

"Do not worry about how you look," the Bush would answer. "You are doing what I need you to do, which is to carry me with you wherever you go."

"How am I doing that?" questioned Butter, somewhat confused.

"You come to drink of my nectar, but it is really my pollen that touches your wings and clings to your feet that is of most importance, for then you spread it about the garden."

Butter felt comforted that she could somehow help the Butterfly Bush, yet she still longed to be as pretty as the rest of her family, especially when her brother, Bellisimo, was about. He would fly above her when she came to drink the bush's sweet nectar and scold her for not being more beautiful.

"You make the crawly things think they can come here whenever they want to drink the nectar meant for us. They see you here in all your plainness and begin to believe they might also be worthy. You must try to make yourself more beautiful so that they understand this bush is only meant for butterflies."

"Why shouldn't they come?" Butter asked in bewilderment. "They can't help being what they are, and maybe if they come and drink the nectar with us they might become beautiful butterflies too."

Bellisimo began to laugh, holding his sides with his wings to stop himself from falling off the twig to which he clung.

"Oh Butter, you are so thick!" came his response. "They can't become butterflies like us, any more than you can become as beautiful as me. We are what we are and can't change into something we aren't."

"We changed from fuzzy worms once didn't we?" Butter pointed out, trying hard to understand what the difference was. Surely if a fuzzy worm could eat itself silly, then go to sleep inside a cocoon and wake up as one of the most beautiful creatures in the garden, it was possible for other creatures to change too.

"That's not the same thing," Bellisimo said in a great huff and fluttered away. He didn't like to be reminded that he hadn't always been beautiful.

"I wonder if butterflies can change into moths

or beetles?" Butter began to ponder, trying hard to understand the mysteries of the garden. "Or flies change into stinging wasps?"

She wanted to know the answer to everything and so went to talk with the other creatures who came to the Butterfly Bush.

"Why do you make sticky strings to crawl on?" she asked one day of the long-legged spider. "It makes the garden all messy."

"It's the only way I can get up from the ground," the long-legged spider responded. "Crawling up the stem would take me forever so I spin my webs and they help me get to where I want to be."

"Where's that?" Butter asked.

"Why the top of the Butterfly Bush, of course. That's where the most beautiful butterflies flutter and they seem so very happy," the long-legged spider replied.

"I can help you," Butter said excitedly. She liked helping others, even if they weren't butterflies, because then she had so many more friends about her. She was a little bit afraid, but she let the long-legged spider crawl

c

onto her delicate wing and then carefully carried him to the top of the Butterfly Bush. He thanked her and began to build himself a web. Butter noticed how the dewdrops in the early morning air seemed to cling to the fine string like hundreds of tiny diamonds reflecting back the brilliance of the sun.

A hard-backed beetle caught Butter's eye and she flew down to where he was trying to crawl up the Butterfly Bush's thick, smooth stem. He would get halfway up and then suddenly tumble back down to the ground. After awhile he would try again, but with the same result. Butter thought she might have given up if it were her making that difficult climb, but the beetle kept trying, over and over again.

"Why do you keep falling off?" she asked him.

"I don't have your wings to carry me to the top of the Butterfly Bush, and I can't make sticky strings like the long-legged spider," he panted, still out of breath from his last tumble. "I only have short, little legs that can barely hold on to the stem so I have to try harder than the rest of you. I might fall more times than most, but I'll get there," he added defiantly.

"Why, I can help you!" Butter said in her usual way. She spread her wings again and the beetle crawled on, admiring their brown, white and blue colouring compared with his own plain, black shell. Butter was startled to hear this because some of her own kind did not think her wings that pretty.

The weight of the beetle was far more than she thought it might be and she had to struggle hard to get to the top of the Butterfly Bush. She was breathless by the time she finally dropped him onto a warm, green leaf, but she couldn't help noticing how the hard-backed beetle's coat of black took on a lovely, lustrous sheen now that he was at the top of the Butterfly Bush.

Butter glanced back at her wings and saw that they had been damaged. One had small rips and tears where the long-legged spider had crawled and the other was sagging and ragged-looking from the weight of carrying the hard-backed beetle. She knew Bellisimo would say she looked worse than ever and wondered how she would explain all this to him.

"Should I worry that he'll send me away from you?"

she asked the Butterfly Bush.

"No one can send you away from me," the Bush replied. "I am here for all, and all may come as best they can. It is good that you work so hard to bring others to me so they too can spread my pollen."

"Well," Butter hesitated, "I do want to help you with that, but I'm afraid I might lose what's left of my wings' prettiness."

The Butterfly Bush didn't respond and so Butter fluttered off, feeling a bit sorry for herself. She found that flying was harder now that her wings were damaged and she was beginning to feel worn out.

A bumbling bee and stinging wasp caught her eye as they circled nearby, buzzing at each other in angry voices as stinging creatures are wont to do. Butter flew over to them to find out why they were arguing.

"Why are you angry?" she asked the two in curiosity.

"What business is it of yours?" demanded the stinging wasp in a surly tone.

"We're arguing over who should get to drink first from the Butterfly Bush's nectar," explained the bumbling bee, who was the kinder of the two. He would only sting others if he felt threatened, unlike the stinging wasp who seemed to do it as often as he could.

"Why don't you both just drink at the same time?" Butter questioned, bewildered by their foolish fight. "There's plenty of nectar to share and I don't think the Butterfly Bush will mind if you drink at the same time. What's important is that you spread his pollen all about the garden."

"How do you know that?" snapped the stinging wasp.

"Why he told me so," explained Butter.

"You can hear him speak?" the bumbling bee asked in awe.

"Of course," the tired little butterfly answered. "Can't you?"

She was having trouble staying aloft and just wanted to go back to the Butterfly Bush and rest awhile. She didn't understand why these two creatures were fighting or why they couldn't hear the Bush speak. Her heart was very big though, and she did want to help, so, despite being tired, she invited them to fly back to the Butterfly Bush with her.

"I've brought two friends with me," she explained to the purple-flowered bush. "Can you tell them about the pollen?"

"You have already told them that," the Butterfly Bush replied. "I will tell them other things they need to know; however, they must stop their buzzing and stinging if they wish to hear my voice."

Butter turned back to the bumbling bee and stinging wasp and was surprised to see that they flew silently together, wing tips almost touching. They stared in wonder at the Butterfly Bush and Butter realized they must have heard its words for not a buzz could be heard. It made her happy to see them flying so close together, nothing but peaceful silence between them.

"I must rest now," thought the tired butterfly and she began to look for a soft leaf on which to lay her head. She picked one and found that it was already occupied by a fuzzy worm that had chewed several holes in the leaf and was now slowly munching it down to nothing.

Butter felt some anger that this crawly thing was eating the green leaves and, for a moment, her face took on that same look worn so often by Bellisimo.

"Why are you ruining the Butterfly Bush?" she asked.

"That spittle bug told me I need to eat leaves so I'll fall asleep and turn into a butterfly. He said the most beautiful butterflies come from cocoons of those who eat the leaves of this bush."

The fuzzy worm waved its squirming body to point to a small bug with very big eyes who gazed at Butter in admiration. It sat on a stem halfway up the Bush and seemed content to stay were it was.

"You are beautiful," mumbled the spittlebug to the plain butterfly.

Butter blushed for she felt uglier than ever before with wings all jagged and torn from the work she had done. She thought about the fuzzy worm trying so hard to become beautiful and, though she felt very tired, decided she must help him before she rested. She gathered as many leaves as she could manage, not worrying about how they stained her wings, and brought them to the fuzzy worm who ate and ate. Finally he stopped eating and began to build a cocoon around himself so that he could become as beautiful as he was meant to be.

Now the day had grown late, the sun had set, and Butter was at the end of her strength. One wing had been broken while gathering leaves and she desperately tried to find somewhere close to rest for she couldn't fly far. She struggled hard, but to her dismay found herself falling and fluttering slowly to the ground. She didn't care what she looked like anymore.

She laid her head on the cold earth and gazed up at the stars that were starting to twinkle in the darkening sky. Above her she could see the silhouette of the Butterfly Bush, its abundant leaves and purple flowers all blending together into a blur as night descended. An earthworm crawled by, seeing neither the Bush nor the helpless butterfly in its blindness. Butter sighed as it went its unseeing way and turned her thoughts instead to all the creatures she had helped bring to the Butterfly Bush. She felt glad that they, at least, had found what they needed and she knew they would help spread its pollen far and wide throughout the garden. With that last thought she fell asleep.

The long, cold night passed and soon the sun was rising, as it always did, making everything new. Its warm light shone down onto the garden and touched the butterfly lying broken on the ground. Butter opened weary eyes to its bright light but had no strength in her to move.

The long-legged spider looked down from where he sat on his newly spun web at the top of the Butterfly Bush and caught sight of her. He realized she couldn't get up and called out as he flung some of his silvery threads to her to try and help, as she had helped him. Butter grasped the sticky silk but was too heavy to climb the thread without breaking it.

The hard-backed beetle saw her too and in dismay tried to find a way down to lend a hand, but his little legs wouldn't allow him to go far. The bumbling bee and the stinging wasp also noticed her lying there and began to buzz all sorts of encouraging words to see if that might give her wings the strength to fly. She nodded back in thanks for their kind concern though it did her little good.

The fuzzy worm woke up and poked his head out from his cocoon. He realized that Butter needed more than words to aid her and so crawled from the comfort of his resting place to chew through the stem of a thick, green leaf, which he then threw down to the ground. She gratefully ate it and it did seem to revive her a little, yet it just wasn't enough.

"Hey, what are you doing down there Butter?" a familiar voice rang out, and there was Bellisimo, yellow wings glowing in the sun.

Butter was too tired to explain, so those she had helped began to call out their stories to him that he might understand why his sister lay broken on the ground. Tears began to fall from Bellisimo's eyes as he listened. He looked back at his own wings and they didn't seem so very beautiful anymore. He flew to his sister and struggled in vain to raise her back up to the Butterfly Bush that she, more than any of them, deserved to be near.

Butter smiled at him, but could not speak for tiredness.

Then the Butterfly Bush spoke and this time all the creatures in the garden could hear him.

"This butterfly gave up the beauty of her wings to help others reach me so that they could help spread my pollen about the garden. Now she is broken and worn, but to me she is the most beautiful of all."

The creatures in the garden began to cheer in agreement and Bellisimo cheered the loudest in praise of all his sister had done.

Butter looked up from the ground where she lay with worn wings all shredded and dull. The Butterfly Bush did not look plain now with the sun shining on its dew-covered leaves and hundreds of butterflies flying above it in joy at its bounty. Indeed it looked more majestic and beautiful than anything else in the garden. Many other creatures had made their way to it to drink of the rich nectar and she saw that it was surrounded by fluttering moths and fuzzy worms, hard-backed beetles and stinging wasps, long-legged spiders, spittlebugs and bumbling bees.

Grasshoppers jumped as high as possible to reach the dark green leaves, while hornets stretched their odd bodies, trying to get as close as they could to the strong

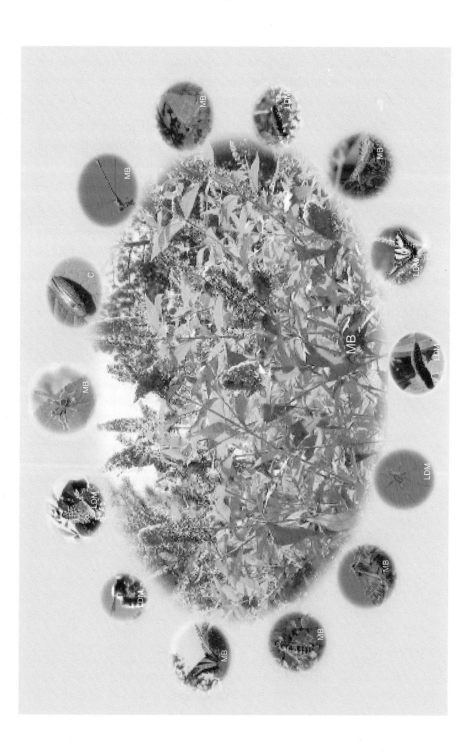

stems. Bug-eyed dragonflies flitted from flower to flower on near-invisible wings, and beetles, bearing coats of many colours, added to the rich medley.

Now the flowers of the Butterfly Bush glowed a more brilliant shade of purple and began to shower down a gentle rain of nectar onto Butter's poor, broken wings.

For a moment she looked as if she might drown beneath the weight of all the Bush was giving her, but instead something strange and wonderful happened.

Her wings began to change and heal. Instead of broken and dull, they became whole and transparent, sparkling like glass in the light. All that remained of her former wings was a tracing of brown and white on the edges, like a silhouette to remind her of how she had once looked.

She spread the lovely, new wings and saw that the sun shone right through them.

With a glad cry Butter took flight, flying straight to the top of the Butterfly Bush where she and her family and friends began to drink together of its plentiful nectar in happy celebration of the new wings that finally matched the beauty of her heart.

Runaway Smudge

A DOG'S LIFE

Just a little dog with a loud bark and not much else to him was probably the best way to describe Smudge. In fact, he was mostly fur, which meant hiding in embarrassment for weeks on end after being taken for his twice-yearly haircut. However, other than having to put up with that humiliation, Smudge had a pretty good life. His days and weeks were filled with delicious dog treats, pats on the head and tummy scratches. As for his joys in life, they matched very closely those in the poem his master had framed and hung on the wall:

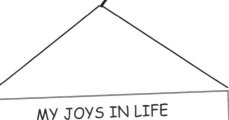

MY JOYS IN LIFE

To chase a ball across the room
To sleep in sunshine 'til high noon
To lick the face of all my friends
To romp and play 'til daytime ends
To eat the scraps upon the floor
To bark at people at the door
To run as fast as ever I can
To lie beneath a scratching hand
To catch a really vicious cat
To sleep 'til morn upon my mat
My joys in life are very few
But, for a dog, a few will do

by: C

The house in which Smudge lived was snuggled cosily into the side of a small mountain on the edge of a forest and had a wide front porch where he often spent his time. Several other houses stood nearby and Smudge liked to watch the different creatures living there, barking at some if they got too close. He never barked at Basher, the big dog who lived next door though; that dog's snarl was as mean as his name. Smudge was so afraid of the big, vicious dog that he would try to make himself even littler, hoping not to be noticed whenever Basher walked by. Smudge much preferred dogs closer to his own size and would wag his tail until it almost fell off whenever any of that sort came by. He wasn't fond of all small animals though. He would bark at birds in the backyard to scare them into flight and chase cats up trees to let them know who was boss. The cats thought him a bit daft, but then they thought that of most dogs.

There was one especially annoying chipmunk who had recently moved into the rock garden in the front yard and he really made Smudge bark in annoyance. When he spotted the small creature he would bark so loud that his master would get angry and call him back into the house.

"We must always consider the neighbours!" he would holler, waggling a finger at the little dog.

This shout was usually followed by an apologetic pat on the head and a delicious dog treat, so Smudge didn't take his master's harsh tone all too seriously. Jester the chipmunk did though. That sound was salvation for him since it meant Smudge would run back into the house, leaving the small chipmunk safe to roam once more. Having begun the hard work of gathering nuts and seeds to store away for the cold winter months, he had to hurry and hide himself whenever the little dog was about. To the chipmunk, Smudge must have seemed like a terrible monster who loved nothing more than making a life, already filled with the struggle of survival, one of constant fear as well.

It was a simple fact that if Smudge ever caught him, the chipmunk would be the one worse for wear.

Now, despite feeling brave when he could bark at things smaller than himself, Smudge didn't feel quite so fearless when the sun set each evening. He'd nervously watch as the shadows grew longer and start to feel very uneasy. Sitting on his comfortable couch, he would hear an unexpected noise and jump up, noticing a shadow move here or there. He'd stare at the spot for a long time, waiting nervously to see if it would happen again. His master would eventually wave a hand in front of the little dog's face and ask him what in the world he was seeing through his doggy eyes. In fact, Smudge didn't really see very well up close, and there wasn't very much to see anyway, except simple shadows. However, since he didn't understand what caused them, his little body would shake with fear and he would sidle up close to his master.

"So much for my guard dog," his master would sigh, yet Smudge took his job of guarding quite seriously. Neither cat nor mouse was going to get into their house unnoticed and live to tell the tale; however, not all creatures who approached the house were cats or mice.

One night, when he and his master were sleeping soundly, Smudge came awake to a great crashing noise. Through the open window he could hear what sounded like an awfully big something snuffling noisily through their garbage bin. Knowing it was his job to guard, he reluctantly rose from his warm bed and headed to his dog door leading to the upper balcony of the house. From there he had a good view of the porch below where the garbage was kept. There were no lights on but the moon was shining brightly.

Unfortunately, while this made it easier to see, it also meant extra shadows, so Smudge was feeling rather nervous as he peeked quietly through the railing.

Garbage tumbling from an overturned bin was the first sight that met his eyes, but there was something else that caused them to widen in shock. Not so very many feet below him was the largest, shaggiest creature he'd ever seen. It stood on four great,

padded feet each showing a number of dangerously sharp claws and, perhaps even worse, a black shadow twice the size of the monster reared up on the garage door beside it.

The creature moved its snout back and forth, as if sniffing the air and Smudge realized it was looking for something. He began to wonder if the creature could climb and hardly had the time to realize he didn't want to find out when the shaggy monster raised its large head, looking straight up into the little dog's eyes.

With a terrified yelp Smudge turned and ran back inside, barking loudly to tell his master to wake up and take over being in charge of guarding the house. Smudge knew his limits.

The next morning Smudge hurried out to the porch, looking about to see if he could spot the huge monster again. There was no visible sign of it. His master had already cleaned away the mess, although Smudge could still smell the scent of the garbage and that of the creature who had been there only a few hours earlier. His nose also told him Jester had been about. Maybe the chipmunk had met up with the monster and...the thought made him grin—at least, that is, until he caught sight of the small chipmunk's head carefully peering out from behind a rock not far away. Their eyes met and Jester's widened in terror. The chipmunk hesitated for half a breath and then whirled in a flash of fur and ran in the direction of his home in the rock wall at the far end of the yard.

Smudge refrained from barking, knowing his master would be straight out to get him if he did. Instead he ran quietly after the chipmunk, determined to put an end to his trespassing. It wasn't really that Smudge was a mean dog, but he'd disliked the chipmunk from the moment he'd decided to move into their yard without asking permission. The little dog swiftly ran the length of the rock wall, coming to a halt when he reached the area where Jester usually disappeared down one hole or another. The dog's nose told him that, for some reason, the chipmunk had bypassed that area today and instead run back toward the house. Following the scent, the dog ran around the yard looking up

trees, over fence posts, behind watering cans, through tall grass and sniffing between rocks until finally he had to sit down and rest.

Plunking himself beside a huge boulder Smudge panted hard, trying to catch his breath. He could still smell the chipmunk, but he didn't seem to be anywhere around, no matter which way the dog looked.

A humming sound from above reached the dog's ears, causing him to look up. There at the top of the boulder was Jester, staring down at him with terrified eyes as big as saucers. With a frightened squeak the chipmunk turned and dashed away. The humming grew louder as Smudge raced to the top of the rock trying to locate the smaller creature. He was just in time to see

Jester's tail disappear down a drainpipe. Smudge peered into the dark hole, unable to see anything except blackness. The humming had followed him and was now right in his ear. The little dog shook his head in annoyance, looking around to see what was causing this bothersome noise.

 # BEE

A bee flew in circles above him, humming with laughter. "Whatever makes you dash about so?" the tiny creature asked, her voice as sweet as honey.

"Jester. He's the chipmunk who steals the seeds we plant to grow vegetables; he's even taking our carrots," Smudge replied with a snap of his jaws to warn the bee to back away. He kept a close eye on her shiny stinger.

"All of them? He must be a huge monster!" she said, wide-eyed with wonder.

"Well no," Smudge admitted. "He's just a small monster with a big appetite. I can't imagine how he eats all the stuff he steals."

"Maybe he's putting it away for the winter to feed his family," the bee buzzed back.

This caused Smudge to pause. He hadn't considered whether the chipmunk might have a hungry family to feed. "Why doesn't he grow his own carrots?" demanded the dog after a moment. "My master works hard to grow the ones we have and then I have to work doubly hard to guard them."

"Maybe he doesn't have a master to help him grow food," the bee suggested.

Smudge hadn't thought of that either. This bee was smart. "Well, who helps you get food?" he asked her in curiosity.

"In the hive we all help each other. I come from a very large family. The sun and rain make the flowers grow and from those we gather nectar to make honey."

"Honey?" Smudge's ears perked up. He'd tasted its sweetness once before when his master had accidentally dropped some on the floor.

"Yes. It takes us many flights and flowers to gather what we need. We bees are very busy. Is your master a human?"

"Yup."

"Oh, then please thank him for all the flowers he plants in your garden. It's the best one around here."

"I'll try," replied Smudge, quite pleased to hear their flower garden was helping others. "Hey, maybe in turn you could sting the big dog next door for us. Basher likes to dig holes in our garden to bury his bones, which makes my master quite cross."

"Why don't you just ask him to stop?" the bee asked, flying in circles above the dog's head.

"I'm afraid of him," Smudge admitted.

"That's probably because you don't understand him."

"What's to understand?" Smudge woofed a bit angrily. "He's just looking for an opportunity to bite someone. None of the other dogs in the neighbourhood like him."

"Hmmm," hummed the bee. "Having no one like me might make me feel pretty angry too."

The serious look on the bee's face made Smudge feel uneasy and he wondered if she was going to sting him. He felt his fur rise in fear and he began to back away.

"Wait!" she called out. "My name's Bastian. What's yours?"

Smudge reluctantly told her his name.

"Well please don't run away, Smudge. I only want to talk with you."

The dog still looked worried, so the bee added:

"I promise not to sting you. We drink the same water that falls from the sky, after all."

"No we don't," Smudge told her. "My water comes from a tap and goes into my dog bowl."

"Really? I thought it all came from the sky. How does it get into your tap?"

"I don't know!" Smudge barked. "It just appears when my master pushes a handle." He was feeling out of sorts because he really had no idea how the water got into the tap and didn't want to look foolish around this tiny bee.

"Well, I think it's a good day if you learn something new," replied Bastian with a beaming smile. "Does your neighbour dog, Basher, get his water the same way?"

"I don't know," Smudge replied. "I guess so."

"You should ask him!" the bee buzzed excitedly. "Maybe we could learn more about this wonderful new source of water!"

"I already told you, he's a mean dog and I certainly won't be stopping by his house to ask him any questions."

"You're that afraid of him?"

"You would be too if you had any sense. Are all bees this silly or is it just you?"

"I may be silly, but I wouldn't let being afraid stop me from finding out something important," Bastian hummed softly.

Smudge lowered his head, feeling rather sorry now for being rude to the bee, who was obviously just a curious sort of creature.

"I could help you learn to be less afraid if you want me to," she coaxed, buzzing in circles about the little dog's head.

Smudge crouched down on his belly, paws covering his ears in a futile effort to hide away from this determined ball of flying fur.

"I see it's not something you're ready to learn right now," Bastian gently droned.

"I am so," Smudge responded, jumping back up. "Only, I'm still afraid you might sting me."

"I'm afraid of that too," admitted the bee. "I won't, though, because stinging you would hurt me even more than it would hurt you."

"It would?" Smudge asked in surprise.

"Indeed yes. You see, I live in a big hive filled with bees. We've learned that stinging usually comes from wanting to keep something we see as ours. If another bee were to try and take it away, we might become angry and buzz very loudly. One angry bee buzzing is bad enough, but when you get two angry bees buzzing at each other, it can lead to stinging and, well..." She drifted off without finishing her sentence, looking a bit sad.

"I guess a whole hive of angry bees buzzing would be the scariest thing of all." Smudge shivered.

"It does make other creatures want to run away," she agreed. "Sometimes we do it because we're afraid someone's trying to steal the honey we need for the long winter months. It's not that we're unwilling to share with others, but more about working together to keep our family safe."

"Does all honey come from bee hives?" Smudge asked, thinking of the honey jar his master kept.

"As far as I know, but I don't know everything. That's why I like to learn new things." Bastian paused to land on a rock close to the dog. "I work really hard at not letting scary things make me sting or fly away because I know I'll end up being sorry later. I won't learn very much if I let that happen."

"That's good to know," Smudge said. He hesitated for a moment then added, "I suppose I should be honest and tell you my master loves honey and eats it all the time from a jar. He gets it from a beekeeper he knows. I got to try it once and I think it tastes almost as good as carrots and dog treats."

"Well, as long as he's not stealing it, but asks the bees' permission, then it's okay. Some bees live in hives humans help build, and in return for all the hard work the humans do to keep the hives safe, the bees allow them to have a share in the honey. We bees have learned that sharing with those who ask is much better than trying to keep everything we have for ourselves, since we almost always get something back in return."

On hearing this Smudge sighed in relief. "Well, thank you for telling me about the hive and especially the honey. It really is delicious."

"There, you see? You just gave me back something in return for the honey."

"I did?"

"Of course! You said thank you and complimented what we bees work so hard to make. Those are the best things we can get back for giving something."

"I never thought of that." Smudge smiled back. "I guess I should thank you for teaching me so much."

"You're welcome. You're teaching me too, you know. So, do you want to learn how to be less afraid?"

The dog nodded and curled himself into a comfortable position to listen to what the bee had to say.

LESSONS
AND IMPORTANT WORDS

Bastian did a quick aerial dance, humming happily to herself for a few moments before coming back to hover in front of Smudge.

"Well, we bees have many lessons to learn. It's the job of the older bees to teach the younger ones all the lessons from the hive," she began. "If we learn them, we'll make fewer mistakes as we buzz through life. Some bees learn fast, others slow, and, sadly, some refuse to learn at all."

"How come?" asked Smudge.

"Because they're afraid of what they might have to give up," she replied. "Remember what I said about how bees buzz in anger when they want to hold on to something they think of as theirs? Well, the harder a bee clings to whatever it's holding onto, the angrier it can get if someone tries to take it away. We already know that if the fear of losing that thing grows too big, it might turn an angry bee into a stinging bee."

"That can't be good," Smudge said with a gulp.

"It's not. If even one bee gives in to this feeling and stings another in anger it can sway other bees to start stinging too. Eventually the whole hive could fall apart."

"Couldn't the bees just fly away?" the dog questioned.

"I suppose they could, but bees don't do very well living away from their hive."

"Well, why can't other bees just stop the stinging?" Smudge asked, scratching his head.

"Once the stinging starts it's very hard to stop," Bastian sighed. "Before you know it bees are either fighting on the side of the one who first stung or the side of the ones who want it stopped. It's bad news for everyone because we end up getting hurt in some way whether we stay and fight or fly away."

"Hmmm," hummed Smudge. "I'm beginning to understand what fear can lead to. Well, I think all the bees should just get together to stop the one who started stinging in the first place."

"Why, what an interesting perspective! We bees hadn't thought of that. Would you mind coming back to the hive and telling the others about it?"

The thought of talking to a swarming mass of bees didn't appeal to Smudge and he shook his head. "You go ahead and tell them for me Bastian."

"Alright," said the tiny bee, and she started to fly away.

"Wait! What does perspective mean?" Smudge called out to her.

The bee stopped in mid-flight and turned back to the little dog. *"Perspective?* Why, it's one of the most important P's of the hive!"

"An important bee? Oh, well, tell them I said hello," Smudge responded.

"No, no! It's not an important bee. It's from lesson P, just like lesson S or lesson H. It's from those lessons taught us by the elder bees to help us survive."

"Oh. So, what does lesson H teach you?" the dog asked.

"You really don't know?" the bee looked shocked. "The three H's teach us the importance of *Hard work, Humility* and *Honey.* Weren't you taught any lessons at all?"

Smudge thought back to some of the things his master had hollered at him over and over again when he was just a young pup. "I think I was, but they weren't called lessons, just important words I needed to know. The three important S words were *Sit*, *Stay* and *Supper*."

"Hmmm. How interesting. I bet your important words are meant to be like our lessons, except dogs and bees need to learn different stuff."

"Really? Why would you think that?" he asked.

"Because a dog's important S words and a bee's lesson S teach very different things. From our lesson S we bees learn to *Seek*, *Sweet*, *Salad*."

"Salad?" Smudge looked bewildered. "I didn't know bees ate salad."

"Umm...we don't. I often get stuck on that last lesson," the bee admitted, flying in worrying circles around a rock.

"Give me a minute," she muttered to herself. "If it's not *Salad*...then, it's *Salamander*...no, that's not it...umm... *Salami*...no, that's not it either. Oh drat! I forget the last one. It's the most important lesson, yet one of the hardest to remember or understand."

She looked so upset at forgetting that Smudge tried to cheer her up by giving a compliment. "My master says it's good to be honest, especially about things we don't understand."

"That's the honest truth, which is why *Truth* is learned in lesson T. Oh, I wish I could remember the last S lesson," she buzzed in frustration.

"What are the other two S lessons about?" the dog enquired, in an effort to take her mind off the forgotten lesson.

It worked beautifully. The bee stopped her frantic flying around the rock and came to hover a few feet in front of the little dog. With a school-teacher-like look on her face, she told him what they meant.

"Bees must seek flowers to find and gather the nectar we

need, and, of course, sweet is the aim of every honey-making bee. Once we know how to find the flowers we then have to learn about the different kinds, when they blossom, how big they get, how long their blooms last, and stuff like that."

"Your lessons sound way too hard for me," Smudge muttered. "Like that one you call perspective, whatever that means. What is it all about anyway?"

"Exactly. Perspective is what it's all about. You understand quite well, I see," the bee replied in admiration, beginning another series of dizzying circles above the poor dog's head.

"Whoa! Stop for a minute, will you?" he begged. "You're giving me a headache with all those loops and back flips, and I still don't get what perspective means."

"Are you telling me you don't understand that it's all about what it's all about?" Bastian buzzed, looking puzzled.

"Huh?" Smudge replied, then gave his head a vigorous shake. "Um...that's exactly what I mean," he continued, saying each word slowly and clearly in hopes that Bastian might better understand him. "Sometimes you talk like you fly, in loops and circles, and that makes me feel confused. It would be easier for me if you just stayed still and got straight to the point so I can figure out what you're trying to say."

"Ah, you need me to make a bee-line!" she shouted, doing several more back flips.

"A what?" Smudge groaned.

"A bee-line," she repeated. "It means going straight there rather than flying in circles—you know, from the hive to the flower and straight back again; no extra stops along the way. Now I get what you need."

The bee hummed happily as she came to hover above the dog, trying hard not to move about, though it wasn't in her nature to stay still for very long.

"Well, a few circles would be okay, if it helps you," Smudge offered, suddenly realizing what a great effort she was making to stay in one place for his sake. Bastian smiled her thanks and began to fly about again, although in a slower manner, with fewer loops.

"Perspective," she began again, "is how I see things and how you see things. No two creatures see things the same way. The best way to learn is by listening to others talk about how they see things from their point of view."

"Oh. Is that hard to do?" Smudge asked.

The bee seemed taken with silent laughter at this simple question. "Sometimes it seems easier when two points of view are very close; however, when they're far apart, then there's work to be done if we really want to understand each other."

"I sort of get what you mean," Smudge said, a bit uncertainly.

"Hmmm..." hummed the bee, as if considering what to say next. "Wait! I have it! What you need is more than just words. Come on, I'll show you instead."

 # FIR

Bastian flew toward a tall fir tree Smudge's master had helped plant at the front of the house when he was just a young boy. It helped shade both the flower garden and the house during the hot summer months. Several bees were busy at work, collecting nectar from the few flowers still blossoming in the late autumn sunshine. Smudge followed, somewhat reluctantly. He wasn't sure if he really wanted to understand anything else today.

"Okay, now walk around it and tell me what you see," the bee commanded as they reached the fir tree's base.

Smudge walked in a wide circle, looking up at the tree's limbs far above his head.

"Do it again. Really look at the branches and the bark," Bastian instructed him.

Smudge obeyed and circled again. He moved closer to it and sniffed, recognizing the scent of Basher, Jester and even that of the strange monster he'd seen the night before. He stared at the branches and noticed they weren't all the same size. He saw that the needles were differing shades, some lighter and some darker, as new growth from last spring joined the older growth from previous years. He told Bastian what he saw.

She looked a bit puzzled when he described the needles as light and dark, since that's not how they looked to her, but only nodded in response.

"What else do you see?" she questioned.

Smudge looked again and saw a bird's nest perched on one of the bigger branches. Cones hung all over the tree, looking similar in shape to the bulbs his master hung from the Christmas tree that was dragged into the house each winter. As the little dog looked up, one of the cones let go of the tree and fell, clonking him soundly on the nose.

"Owwwoof! That hurt!"

Bastian flew to where Smudge sat rubbing his paws over his muzzle to take away the ache.

"Are you okay?" she enquired.

The little dog nodded.

"Well that cone never meant to hurt you, but it did. It had to fall and you just happened to be at the wrong place at the wrong time."

"Yup," Smudge groaned, still rubbing at his nose.

"That reminds me of the frog I saw a few nights ago. My master and I had stepped outside for a minute when we suddenly heard the hissing of a snake. We ran back into the house and looked through the window to see if we could spot it, and that's when we saw the frog. It was hopping after us as fast as it could—making a bee-line toward the back door you might say." He woofed in laughter at his own joke. "The poor thing was no bigger than a leaf, and shook like one too, it was so scared. It stopped for a moment and we spotted the snake moving over a rock toward it.

I guess the frog saw it too because it made a frantic leap toward the door and pressed hard against it. I guess it didn't want to be the snake's supper and had the most frightened look on its face. My master said he could almost hear the frog crying 'help, help'. I don't think my master hears very well because the frog was clearly saying 'save me please!' in that deep, rib-it-ing voice they have."

"Hmmm. Sort of the same thing," the bee droned. "That snake probably wasn't trying to be mean to the frog any more than the pine cone was trying to be mean to you. I bet the snake was just as afraid of starving to death as the frog was of being eaten."

"I guess they were only thinking of themselves," sighed Smudge.

"That's often what fear is about. So, are you still mad at the pine cone?" Bastian asked.

Smudge laughed and shook his head to say no.

"And do you think you understand this tree now?" the bee continued.

"Sure. It's fat at the bottom and has lots of branches at the top. It makes nice shade to sit beneath on a hot day and drops pine cones from time to time."

"How does it smell?"

"Well, kind of like plant things do, but also like Jester and some of the other creatures that live around here."

"You mean like the ants crawling up its bark and the birds who perch in its branches?"

"No, I mean like the monster who knocked over our garbage last night, and Jester, and the big dog next door. I never thought about ants and birds."

"And I never thought about dogs and chipmunks until you mentioned them," replied Bastian. "We think we're looking at the tree in the same way, but we don't all see the same picture or smell the same scents. You can only see it from the ground, whereas I can also see it from the air or can land on a branch and look around from there." The bee flew to one of the lower branches to make her point, then zoomed high into the air and landed on the topmost branch of the fir. "I might be able to understand the tree from your perspective if you let me sit on your nose while you walk around it, Smudge," she shouted down to him. Without waiting for a response, the tiny creature flew back down and landed on the dog's black nose.

This time Smudge didn't flinch. He was beginning to trust his new friend, who was actually very likeable—not at all what he'd expected of a bee. Smudge walked several times around the tree, moving close under its dark, heavy branches, and then standing back to gaze up so the bee could see it at the same angle he did.

"Thank you," said Bastian, launching off the dog's nose and buzzing away again. "Now I understand a bit better how you see this tree. It's harder for you to see it from my perspective though, since you don't have wings to fly. I'm willing to let you sit on my nose if you want to, although I expect a monster of your size would squish me." She flew a zigzag pattern above the dog, grinning widely.

"Maybe I shouldn't sit on your nose, Bastian," he snickered in reply, "but I think I do understand more of your point of view now."

"Well, even though I sat on your nose, I don't have your eyes, so I still didn't see the tree exactly as you do," she hummed. "I suppose if we were meant to see it the same way we would have all been given the same eyes."

"Do you think that's the only reason we have different eyes?" the dog asked.

"Well, one of them anyway. Our queen bee says that, with the sky being so big, the rain so plentiful, the flowers so many and the sun so bright, we'd have to live forever to learn everything there is to know about each one of them. Maybe we're given different eyes to help each other see what's too big for any of us to see alone."

"Your queen sounds pretty smart," said Smudge, "but I'm sorry to say my master doesn't care for your kind overly much. He says there are more dratted bees in his garden than raindrops in a cloudburst. I think he's wrong, because I've tried counting raindrops and there just aren't enough numbers to count them all."

"Some creatures make things seem way bigger than they are when they talk about what scares them," Bastian droned. "For myself, I think it's much less scary to look at them as they really are, although even that can change depending on where I am. This tree seems very big when I'm up close to it and much smaller when I fly farther away. Fear can be like that too. As for your human, he's probably more afraid of our stingers than of us. You've made me feel a bit sad though. I really thought your human had planted this beautiful flower garden because he liked us." She hung her head and tears started to form in her eyes.

"Oh please don't be sad," Smudge begged. "I used to think bees were scary too. Maybe if my master gets to know you he'll like you better." The little dog looked back at the fir tree, wondering now if it was truly as tall as it appeared to be through his eyes. "You know, I think you're quite wise, Bastian. I thought I really understood this tree, but now I realize for that to be true I'm going to have to learn to see it through the eyes of others as well. I suppose I'll need to find out what they smell, hear and taste too if I really want to understand it completely."

"I'm no wiser than anyone else who's willing to open their eyes to see as much as they can," replied the humble bee.

"Once you learn someone else's point of view, you understand them better and they don't seem quite as scary," Smudge noted.

"That's right," Bastian chimed. "It's not always easy though, and many creatures don't make time to do it."

Smudge thought about Jester hurrying to store nuts and roots for his family before the coming winter. "They're probably too busy with important things like finding food and keeping warm," he said, with a sudden feeling of guilt that all he had to do to get food was guard the house and garden, and wag his tail whenever his master was about. He began to consider whether he should start sharing some of his food with the chipmunk so Jester wouldn't have to work so hard to stay alive. The little dog realized he might have some trouble explaining this to his master though. The man might be upset if his guard dog just sat and watched while chipmunks raided their garden. He told Bastian about how he wanted to help the chipmunk and about his problem.

"Is your master the kind of creature who wants to understand others?" Bastian questioned.

"I'm not sure," Smudge slowly replied. "I think he tries to understand me, although he doesn't speak dog language. Oh, he gets tail wagging well enough. Who doesn't? But he sure doesn't understand what barking means. You'd think I was the only one who could see all the birds, cats and mice that come sneaking into our yard. Anyway, when he doesn't like something he doesn't easily change his mind about it. For instance, he often says he'll never understand neighbours who don't pick up after their dogs. To be honest, I have to admit I don't get why he bothers picking up after me at all. Just leave it on the ground, I say. What do you think, Bastian?" He asked this in an anxious voice.

"I think when someone says they'll never understand they usually mean they don't want to at that moment. Your human probably isn't ready yet or else he doesn't have the time."

"He is pretty busy," Smudge said, trying to defend his master, "but I don't know for sure if that's the reason. Maybe he's afraid that if he looks at things from someone else's perspective he'll lose his own. You did say that bees get angry when they're trying to hold onto something they want to keep. I wonder if it's the same for humans."

"I think it's that way for most creatures," Bastian sighed. "We bees get angry when others try to steal from us, just like you with the chipmunk. Don't feel bad about your master though. Some bees work side by side all their lives and still can't find time to learn each other's point of view." Bastian glanced over at the flower garden where her fellow bees continued to extract nectar from the brightly coloured flowers. "Even creatures with wings to fly or the ability to see more than others might never understand this tree to the fullest. It's all because they refuse to look at it from different angles and through other's eyes."

"My master says you can't teach an old dog new tricks, but he's wrong," yapped Smudge. "I'm nearly nine and I've just learned the trick of seeing things through a bee's eyes."

"Very good," Bastian praised him. "Do you think you're ready to learn the second of the bees' three P's?"

Smudge nodded. He'd thoroughly enjoyed his morning with the bee and was looking forward to putting the first P lesson to good use. No point in learning a lesson if you didn't use it after all. A dragonfly chose that moment to swoop over his head and landed neatly on the warm pavement beside him. Smudge followed its lead and sat down on the ground, now nicely heated by the sun.

"Hello," Smudge called out to the dragonfly.

The long-winged bug didn't seem inclined toward conversation and immediately took off again. Smudge shrugged and settled himself more comfortably on the ground, waiting for the bee to continue.

DOGGEDNESS

Smudge watched as Bastian flew to a nearby flower of brilliant yellow and settled herself on its delicate petals. It moved slightly under her weight as she walked toward a small drop of water that had been left behind by the morning dew and sipped delicately of the shining liquid.

She was soon refreshed, and turned back to Smudge.

"The second P lesson isn't an easy one to say," she warned him.

"Nothing can be harder than perspective," Smudge snickered.

Bastian gave a sharp buzz in response to the interruption.

"Sorry Bastian. Go ahead," Smudge said, settling down to listen.

The bee folded her wings back and, with her best schoolteacher look, slowly said: *"Perseverance."*

"Whoa! I'll never be able to say that!" Smudge exclaimed.

"Perhaps if you work hard at trying to say it you'll eventually get it right," encouraged Bastian with a chuckle.

"Humph. I don't think so, but I'll try," he agreed, looking less than hopeful.

Bastian said the word again and Smudge repeated it after her. After many more tries, and just when the little dog was about ready to give up, he finally got it right.

"Perseverance!" he shouted, feeling quite pleased with himself. "Now tell me what it means."

"Why, it means the same thing as persistence," Bastian grinned

Smudge gave a loud groan. "And what does that mean?"

"It means to keep trying something until you get it right; to keep going even when something is hard. Learning another perspective can be very difficult for a bee, which is why we need perseverance to go with it. It basically means not giving up."

"I can appreciate why it's such an important lesson," said Smudge. "Is there anything else I should know about it?"

"Well, you've already learned what's most important," teased Bastian, "but maybe I should tell you it also means the same thing as doggedness."

"Woof!" laughed Smudge. "Now you're speaking a language I can understand!" He gave his tail a happy wag. "Okay, let's hear that final P lesson."

"Oh my, look at how high the sun has risen in the sky!" Bastian suddenly exclaimed. She launched herself off the flower and into the air. "I have so much work to do. I'd almost forgotten. Better make a bee-line for the hive. I'm afraid you'll have to wait until tomorrow for the answer, Smudge. Good-bye! See you soon!"

"No wait!" he called after her, but it was too late.

The babbling bee had flown straight out of sight. Smudge sighed. He didn't want to wait until tomorrow to find out the last part of lesson P. Feeling a bit disgruntled, he headed for the front porch. The light of the noonday sun on his back made his fur look more silver and grey than black and white, and the sun's warmth made him think of a nice, long nap. He gave a great stretch and yawn. As he scratched at a flea biting him in the most annoying fashion behind his left ear, he suddenly remembered Jester. Rising again, he headed to the vegetable garden, pulled a couple of choice carrots from the soft earth and dropped them by the drainpipe where he'd last seen the chipmunk.

"Jester, these are for you," he called out in the kindest voice he could manage. There was no response. "Hey, Jester, I have carrots to help you feed your family," he barked a bit louder.

Further silence followed this second offer. Smudge decided not to feel hurt, since he now understood the chipmunk's perspective a bit better. He couldn't really blame the small creature for not trusting him, since he hadn't exactly gone out of his way to be the chipmunk's friend. Well, Bastian had said perspective needed perseverance, so Smudge decided not to give up. He would just keep sharing some of his food everyday until the chipmunk finally started to trust him. That odd feeling of happiness, which seemed to come whenever he gave to others, began to warm Smudge on the inside. He wandered back toward the front porch again, quite ready for a long nap.

 # BEAR

Smudge spent several minutes finding just the right position for an afternoon snooze and had hardly settled into a comfortable spot when he gave a start and sat back up. A brown head had suddenly appeared coming over the mountain, followed by a huge, shaggy body. The monster he'd seen the night before!

The creature ambled slowly into sight, nosing here and there as he poked along. Smudge watched him make his way down the road, coming closer and closer to the driveway. The little dog stayed very still, trying hard to make himself invisible, as he usually did when afraid—and, as usual, it didn't work. The monster just kept coming. Smudge was terrified and wanted to run into the house, but his job was to guard, even if it meant protecting their dirty, old garbage bin, which had already been moved to the safety of the garage. A greyish ball of fur and fury, he went racing down the driveway barking loudly at the intruder. He was amazed to see how huge the beast was up close and how sharp his claws really where.

The brown monster pulled back for a moment, probably more in puzzlement at what all the barking was about then in fear. After a moment, he gave a rough growl, as if clearing his throat.

"Are you a rat or a hedgehog?" the monster demanded.

Smudge's barking spluttered to a halt and he sat down in surprise. Never in his life had anyone called him a rat! "I'm a dog!" he barked indignantly, forgetting to be afraid. "Have you never seen a dog before?"

"Of course. But you're such a little one I wasn't really sure," the monster replied.

"Humph!" Smudge responded with a sniff. "And what kind of creature are you?"

"I'm a bear. Haven't you ever met a bear before?"

"No, I haven't," Smudge admitted. "Which house do you and your master live in?"

"What's a house and what's a master?" the bear asked, confused.

Smudge looked hard at the bear and realized he really didn't know.

"A house is the big wooden thing behind us. I live there and it's warm and comfortable inside."

"Like a cave?" the bear asked.

"Sort of—and a master is someone who gives you food, teaches you what's right and what's wrong, and scratches you in spots you can't reach. If you don't have a master, who gives you food? Does your family get it for you?"

"I live alone and get my own food," the huge bear rumbled, sounding envious. "I eat berries in the summer and salmon that swim the rivers in the fall."

"What about winter and spring? And what would you eat if the berries didn't ripen and there were no salmon in the rivers?" Smudge asked several questions all at once, suddenly full of curiosity about this strange creature's way of life.

"I sleep during the winter and in the spring eat anything I can get; and, of course, I eat honey whenever I can steal it from those horrible bees. It tastes better than all the salmon and berries put together. Oh, and sometimes humans are kind enough to put out food for me. In fact, I found some here last night. When I can't find anything to eat, I get very grumpy," he added with a huffy growl, looking quite cross.

Smudge felt rather sorry for the huge creature when he heard this. At least now he understood why the bear had gone searching through their garbage. He thought again about Jester having to gather food for himself and his family. The little dog was beginning to realize just how much effort went into feeding oneself. With this came a new appreciation for the work his master did to earn all those dog treats, and Smudge resolved to be a better guard dog in future. He'd do what he could to help earn his share of the food. Maybe he could dig up his master's garden and bring all the vegetables into the house for him. Surely his master would appreciate that! Smudge looked more kindly at the bear now, realizing that life in the wild must get pretty cold and hungry at times, and lonely too if there was no family or master to love. Not having food when you needed it suddenly seemed a terrible thing to the well-fed dog. Still, not having something you needed didn't make it right for you to steal it from someone else. The part about stealing from the hard-working bees really bothered Smudge. He decided to tell the bear about Bastian.

"I have a bee friend," he said aloud.

"A what?"

"A bee friend. A friend who is a bee."

"A bee friend!" The bear began to shake with laughter. "No one with any sense has a bee friend! Don't you know bees can sting?"

"Bastian wouldn't sting me," Smudge replied with confidence. "She's very kind, and we talk about all sorts of interesting things."

"Well, off course a bee wouldn't sting you unless it was afraid of you...or very angry. They're likely to die once they use their stinger."

"What? I don't believe you!" Smudge barked in disbelief.

The bear chuckled. "How could you have a bee friend and not know something as important as that? You aren't very smart, are you? Well, now you know, so don't go making her angry or you'll both be sorry."

"I may not be as smart as you think you are," Smudge replied, feeling much less sorry for the bear, "but at least I understand that if you make friends with a bee you're far more likely to get some of her honey! And that's far better than stealing it."

Now it was the bear's turn to sit back on his haunches in surprise. He scratched his head, as if trying to make sense of what he'd just heard. After a few minutes of grunting and snuffling, he raised his huge form again and looked down at the little dog.

"Well, I think you just might be right. I don't know how a bear and bee could ever be friends, though; but I suppose it may be possible. I'm glad I stopped to talk to you. Your barking scared me at first, and I did consider swatting you away, but now I'm glad I didn't."

"I was pretty scared too," Smudge admitted, secretly thrilled to learn such a huge creature had been frightened of him. "I usually feel brave if I bark loud and make others run away. When you didn't, I almost turned and ran away myself, but I'm glad we had a chance to get to know a bit about each other. Maybe I'll see you again sometime."

"Sure," nodded the bear with a lopsided grin. "You can teach me more about bee friends and masters."

The little dog responded by wagging his tail in friendship.

The bear gave a nod, then turned his huge, furry frame around, waddling up the road, and continuing on even higher until he reached the forest at the top of the small mountain.

Smudge watched the bear's slow progress as he climbed back over the mountain from where he'd come. The little dog spent the rest of the day feeling quite happy, thinking about his new friends. He'd learned so much, and felt braver then ever before. Now the daytime shadows made him laugh, and he even found himself gazing fondly at his own grey companion stretched out below him on a rock. As it began to lengthen with the setting sun, he hopped about to amuse his master, who had come outside to join him. The man sat in a large chair, chuckling out loud as he watched the long shadow cast by his little dog doing wild, tail-chasing spins.

They spent the evening curled up by the fireplace, enjoying the warmth of burning logs, and, even though it was dark, with his master close by, Smudge was hardly feeling afraid at all. He thought about how wonderful it would be to never be afraid again and wondered if he could really learn how. There was no way a frog could look a snake in the eye and not be afraid, knowing he might soon be supper; but then Smudge recalled what Bastian had said about the frog and snake both being afraid, which made sense.

A log suddenly crackled on the fire, interrupting his thoughts. Sparks flew everywhere before the fire finally settled back down; however, it was enough to make the shadows flare, and the little dog felt a moment of fear. He shivered and sidled closer to his master for protection. As the shadows grew small again, Smudge gave himself a shake. He looked over to the fireplace, watching the wood glow a bright red. It brought to mind the fir tree he'd studied so carefully that morning and he began to wonder if a tree could feel fear, and whether it would be afraid of a human coming to chop it down with an axe.

He'd have to ask Bastian the next time she flew by.

TO BE A TREE

The next day started out much the same as the last. Smudge had risen early and begun his morning by barking at a few birds in the backyard before enjoying a good breakfast of scraps from the table. Toast with marmalade and a good chunk of cheese suited him just fine, but he remembered the chipmunk's family and set aside a nice bit of the seed-covered crust. His master had decided to read up on the habits of bears and kindly took the time to explain it all to Smudge. He told him how bears could become confused if they thought they could get free food from garbage bins and said that, when it came to food, bears were awfully quick learners.

Smudge wasn't let outside until about mid-morning. He immediately rushed to where he'd left the carrots the day before. They were gone. He laid down the piece of crust saved from breakfast and called out for Jester to come and take it whenever he liked. That business finished, the little dog then trotted to the front of the house, where the bees were already busy at work in the flower garden. Smudge wandered over to the patch of brightly coloured blossoms wondering how he'd ever be able to find Bastian amongst the flurry of tiny bodies flitting here and there. He needn't have worried, though, for one of the buzzing balls suddenly rose up and flew directly at him.Smudge couldn't help yelping and backing away. It was hard not to snap his jaws in fear at the tiny bee.

"Wait! It's me," the bee called out, and then Smudge recognized his friend.

"Hi Bastian! Sorry about that. I'm sure glad I didn't bite you."

"So am I," she grinned.

"It's hard not to, even when you know you shouldn't," Smudge noted.

"Too true," Bastian agreed. "I feel the same way about stinging, but it does get easier if you practice saying no to yourself."

"That's good to know," Smudge sighed. "I think it's going to take loads of practice for me to get good at it. Hey Bastian, I'm really glad you came back. I can't wait to find out about your third P lesson."

"You're a bit impatient, Smudge. Does that help you guess what the lesson might be?" she asked as she finished a back flip.

"Nope," Smudge promptly replied. "I don't like guessing. It takes too long. Just tell me, okay?"

The bee gave a loud buzz of laughter as she circled above her four-legged friend. "It's *Patience.*"

Smudge turned several shades of red beneath his soft coat of fur. "Oh...er...I suppose that means I need more of it."

"We all do if we want to understand others and want them to understand us. It takes patience and perseverance to learn different perspectives." She grinned and went zipping wildly about her friend's head.

"Stop Bastian! You're making my head hurt!" Smudge shook himself all over, like a dog does when it's wet. "I wish there weren't so many big words in your lessons. I think I'm going to have to learn to use my master's dictionary."

"His what?" the bee asked, looking bewildered.

"His dictionary. It's a book where all the words in the world are kept so you can find out what they mean. My master says when we're small we don't always understand words, but when we grow bigger we understand more. I'm not so sure he's right about that, though, because you're way smaller than me and still know more big words than I do."

"All the words are in there?" the bee questioned greedily,

her eyes bugging out in excitement. "It sounds wonderful, but...what's a book?"

"It would take way too long to explain. I'd have to show you one. All you need to know for now is that there are heaps of them and they're made of paper, which comes from trees. Everything you ever wanted to know is in them."

He looked to see if Bastian was impressed with his knowledge, and she was indeed looking wide-eyed with wonder. Smudge felt quite proud of himself and couldn't help adding: "Each one is different, and together they hold all the knowledge in the world. The dictionary tells about words, but other books tell about animals, stars, far away places and all sorts of other stuff. There's even one that has all the answers and only waits for us to ask the right questions—at least, I think that's what my master said. I'm hoping I'll grow bigger because I really want to look in that one. I have so many questions." He finished with a sigh.

"It sounds almost too good to be true!" Bastian quivered. "Of course, there are other things I used to think sounded unbelievable until I came to understand them."

"Like what?" Smudge asked, watching the bee land on another flower. When he saw her begin to gather nectar he added: "I hope I'm not keeping you from your work, Bastian."

The tiny creature smiled in reply. "I'll be back in a bit," she said, and zoomed out of sight.

Smudge curled up on the warm ground and laid his head down, content to take a bit of a nap while waiting for Bastian's return. It was a pleasant day, with a sky mostly free of clouds, except for one dark patch sitting on the horizon. However, it was far enough off that the little dog wasn't too worried about rain.

"Funny how one can like to drink water yet hate to get wet," he thought drowsily.

"So tell me about how this paper stuff comes from trees."

The unexpected buzz in his ear caused Smudge to leap so high that he had to give a quick twist to make sure he didn't land on his back. As it was, he still landed in a rather awkward heap.

"I didn't think you'd get back so fast," he grumbled, picking himself up and pretending he'd meant to land that way.

"I'm sorry if I scared you," Bastian apologized.

"That's okay. I wasn't really scared, just startled. And sorry, but I can't really tell you how paper works. I don't know much about it except that humans take trees and somehow turn them into paper."

"Humans are awfully clever," Bastian noted.

As she hovered in front him, Smudge noticed the bee's pollen basket was empty and that there was no sign of the nectar she'd gathered from the flowers. "She certainly is a busy bee," he thought, feeling grateful that she was willing to share her precious time with him. Aloud he said: "Hey Bastian, last night we had some logs burning in the fireplace and it got me thinking." He quickly told her about the tree and the man with the axe. "So, what I want to know is, how could anyone want to understand our perspective if it's opposite to theirs? Why would a tree bother trying to understand a man with an axe if it knew the human was going to hurt it by chopping it down?"

"I'm not sure," the bee slowly answered. "I guess it's the same thing as a frog bothering to try and understand why a snake wants to eat it for supper. Better for the frog to run away and be safe, but better for the snake to catch the frog and not starve."

"The frog will probably end up being somebody's supper anyway," Smudge pointed out.

"True. It likely spends much of its life hiding away, but would probably live more peacefully if it just accepted what was going to happen in the end. Maybe then it wouldn't be so afraid when the end did come about."

Smudge thought about this for a few minutes, struggling to understand the point she was making. "Hey Bastian, do you think we might all need each other somehow, even if we don't realize it or like it? Maybe there's a balance we don't understand yet, which says one creature has to have supper and the other has to be supper for the whole thing to work."

"Hmmm, you might be onto something, Smudge. If the frog really wanted to help the snake, it could give itself up for supper without being mad at it."

"And if the snake wanted to help the frog, it could choose to starve rather than harm the frog," Smudge concluded, "or at least feel sorry for hurting it."

"I think that answers your question about the tree and the man with the axe," Bastian noted. "The reason we need to try to understand another creature's perspective, even when it's opposite to our own and might hurt us, is so that we won't feel angry with them even when we don't agree with them."

"Which doesn't mean we won't feel scared," Smudge put in, thinking of Basher. He gave a big stretch, his little body suddenly looking much longer and slimmer, and his padded paws stretched out in all directions. "I guess understanding and agreeing aren't exactly the same thing."

The tiny bee flew over and perched once more on the end of the little dog's cold, shiny nose, and peered into his dark eyes. "You're very smart, Smudge."

"Me?" Smudge asked. "Not really." He felt quite pleased by the bee's compliment, but he wasn't so sure she was correct. "My master's pretty smart, though. He says if you want to be unhappy for the rest of your life, just stay angry."

"Your human sounds more like a bee every time you mention him. I'd love to bring the whole hive over to meet him," Bastian buzzed enthusiastically.

"Um, maybe you'd better wait for an invitation. He doesn't like unexpected company." Smudge imagined how upset his master would be if he saw a swarm of bees at his door.

"Oh, okay. We'll just wait for him to ask us over," she replied.

Smudge gave a soft sigh of relief, but the bee didn't seem to notice. A few other bees had flown over for a quick chat with Bastian, and the group literally hummed with liveliness as they flew about the poor dog's head. After a bit they buzzed off and Bastian launched herself from the dog's nose and flew up alongside the fir tree's tall trunk. Smudge sighed in relief as she left him. As much as he'd come to like the tiny bee, it still made him feel a bit cross-eyed to have her so close.

"Wouldn't it be great if we could just turn into another creature whenever we needed to understand it better?" she asked him.

Smudge had followed her and began to circle the enormous tree's base, looking up into its thick branches as if trying learn all he could about it. "It sure would," he replied, "but I'd be happy enough if the tree could just talk to us so we could ask it questions and learn its perspective."

"Perhaps their way of speaking is bending in the wind, reaching up toward the sky and putting down roots that entwine with other plants," Bastian suggested. "Hey, Smudge, do you known how this tree got planted here?"

"I think my master's father planted it there to give shade in the summer. My master gives it water when the weather is hot and plant food to help it grow taller and stronger."

"I wondered why it looked so much healthier than some of the other trees growing on the mountain. They do seem to do better when humans take care of them. I bet this tree would have a different point of view about your master coming to chop it down if it could realize it had been planted for a purpose."

"You mean it might feel it sort of owed thanks to my master for all it had been given?"

"Yes. I guess the tree would have to decide whether the gift of being planted and cared for was worth the price of being chopped down in the end for firewood...or paper."

The bee flew in a slow circle around the little dog's head, adding: "Perhaps the best we can hope for is to figure out why we've been planted here and then decide how we're going to act when another creature needs us."

"If I knew someone needed me, and they asked nicely, I'd want to help," Smudge stated firmly.

"Ah, but what if they needed you and just didn't know it? What if they snarled at you like that big dog next door?" Bastian questioned.

"I guess I'd run away," Smudge admitted. "I thought you said you could help with that."

"I can tell you that running away when you're afraid doesn't make you less afraid. In fact, if you stop running, face what you're afraid of and try to understand it, you'll find yourself far less afraid."

"Even if it bites me?" Smudge inquired.

"Yes, even if it bites you," Bastian confirmed. "Most of the time you'll find the bite doesn't hurt half as much as being afraid all the time. As for not being afraid at all, well, I suppose it would take quite a bit of understanding to stop being afraid completely."

"I guess the best thing to do if you're afraid is to step back for a bit without barking or biting," Smudge suggested.

"Or stinging," Bastian agreed. "At least until you have a chance to learn the other creature's point of view."

"Yup. I still don't like Basher's point of view though," the little dog growled, "which is why I take several big steps back when he's around. I've been practising making myself invisible."

"Ah yes," the bee nodded, "except that, when you pretend you aren't there, others might feel sad or mad because you're ignoring them. When they feel hurt, some creatures want to hurt back."

"He scared me first!" Smudge stated, defending himself; "and if Basher wants to ignore me, that's just fine."

"Well, he didn't know you before he didn't like you, so something must have happened when you first met."

Smudge scratched vigorously at another pesky flea, which had stopped to take a bite out of his back. "Not that I remember," he replied, thinking back to his first meeting with the big dog. "I walked by his house and saw him on the porch, so thought I should introduce myself. Before I'd taken more then a few steps into his yard he started to snarl. I got scared and ran away. Since then, whenever he sees me he snarls and I do my best to disappear. I'm not very good at it," he admitted sadly.

"I wonder if Basher acts that way because he's been hurt before and is afraid it'll happen again," Bastian mused.

"Now you sound like my master," Smudge barked. "He says Basher must have got kicked quite hard as a puppy to be such a mean old dog."

"Hmmm...your master does sound smart. Humans are the ones who first approached the bees to make friends, you know. They've helped us build bigger, better hives in return for sharing our honey. It took some bees quite awhile to put away their stingers and see that we could make way more honey if we worked together."

"Yup, humans can be really helpful when they want," Smudge agreed. "But Basher is a different story. Just because bad stuff happens doesn't make it okay to snarl at everyone. How am I supposed to find a way to get along with him if he acts like he wants to bite my head off all the time?"

"You'll have to ask Basher that question. Until you do, you won't really know if he snarls because he wants you to pay attention to him or to make you run away."

Smudge stood up and began to wander down the driveway. Bastian flew alongside him, as if anxious not to lose her new friend. They stopped about halfway down the paved sloped so the little dog could sniff the tall stalks of wild grass growing beside it. The grass had long since dried up in the sun and Smudge caught the lingering scent of the brown monster against its rough edges.

"Oh, I forgot to tell you about the bear," he said to Bastian, and shared the story of the garbage and the unexpected meeting with her. "When he came into my yard, I barked at him, but I got scared when he didn't leave. I almost ran away, but then I remembered how scared I felt when I first met you and decided to stay and talk with him. After a bit he didn't seem so scary anymore, and I even learned some new stuff." The dog sniffed again at the withered vegetation on the side of the driveway, thinking of what the huge creature had said before waddling away. "I think he may have learned a few things too."

"What a brave thing to do!" the bee exclaimed.

"Me..? Brave..?" Smudge felt a rush of pride. No one had ever called him brave before.

Sure," Bastian said. "Not running away from what scares us is what being brave is all about. Remember, you didn't run away from me either, even though I had a stinger. I don't think you realize how brave you really are."

"Well, I'm glad I didn't run away from you. If I had, I wouldn't have learned all those lessons," Smudge replied, "and now we're friends, so I know you won't sting me."

"Not on purpose," Bastian said with a serious look on her face, "but even friends can hurt each other without meaning to."

"Well, as long as you told me you were sorry, I wouldn't be mad for long," said Smudge, reassuring the bee with a smile.

"What about Basher? If you knew he was sorry, would you still ignore him?"

"I don't know," grumbled Smudge, the smile disappearing again. "Probably not." He heaved a sigh, adding, "I suppose Basher doesn't like to be ignored, but he can't expect us to be friends if he's going to snarl every time he sees me."

"Of course not," Bastian agreed. "Maybe he's just trying to make himself scary so nobody hurts him. Fear can be about not wanting to lose something, but it can also be about being pushed into taking something we don't want. If someone pushes us so hard that we finally have to stand up for ourselves, we may want to make sure nobody ever pushes us again. It's times like that when a good bee can turn into an angry bee and then most everyone wants to run away. It takes someone pretty brave to stand up to an angry bee's sting."

"I see your point," Smudge nodded. "Perhaps it's best not to run or fight when we're afraid. Perhaps we need to try and figure out what makes someone want to sting or bite us in the first place and then maybe we can find a way to make peace. Of course, that would take patience." Smudge sighed as if that was something he thought might be beyond hope.

"Sounds like a great idea, but it's harder for some of us than others," Bastian sympathized. "Some creatures are patient because they're made that way, but I'm sure not. I had to practise pretty hard to get good at it. Even now, waiting isn't easy when I want to get work finished and there's something in my way. The other bees say I get really buzzy, which used to make me even buzzier. I finally realized I needed to think about what they said instead of just getting mad at them. I guess we're better at seeing what others need to change than at seeing what we need to change in ourselves."

"Being honest with myself can be as hard as being patient," Smudge admitted.

"Too bad we aren't born knowing all our lessons; then we might never hurt anyone at all." Bastian flew high into the air at the thought and began one of her aerial dances.

Smudge took the opportunity to look over a nearby clump of grass in hope of finding some live, soft blades to nibble. To his delight, he found a few still remained hidden deep within a dried yellow bunch. He pulled them out and leisurely began to chew them.

 # **LESSON C**

Watching Bastian flying in zigzag patterns high above him was rather interesting, and Smudge could hear her softly humming several lines to herself. He waited patiently until she finished and came flying back to him again.

"Lessons from the hive," she explained. "Smudge, I was thinking. Wouldn't it be nice if we could just undo our mistakes?"

"It sure would," he agreed. "There are some days I wish I could do over again."

"I know what you mean," Bastian nodded. "In the hive we call those *learning days*."

"They often feel more like a learning *daze* to me," Smudge chuckled.

Bastian grinned appreciatively and did an enormous double-loop back flip in the air. She ended by coming to hover in an awkward, wrong-side-up position in front of the dog. Seeing the bee hanging upside down made Smudge feel a bit unsteady and he tilted his head as far as he could to one side so he could see her from a better angle. She winked a tiny eye and began to drone in a singsong voice a recital of the lesson she had learned.

> *"We **can't** go back and **change** the past*
> *Not even if we fly quite fast*
> *But only forward **can** we go*
> *To **change** the future, and we know*
> *By changing what we do right now*
> *Takes **courage** that could then allow*
> *A **consequence** that's good or bad*
> *(Though hard ones, too, can make us glad).*
> *If we decide we want to be*
> *A creature that can truly see,*
> *We choose the **choice** that helps us grow*
> *And to the bad ones, we say no!"*

"The C Lessons?" the dog enquired.

The bee flashed him another grin.

"Can, Can't, Change, Choice, Courage and **Consequence—** all start with the letter C, though you can't hear the sound of the sea in any of them!" Bastian laughed.

"Um...what?" Smudge asked in confusion.

"Oh, it's just a silly bee joke. I've been told it doesn't hold much water."

Smudge tilted his head to one side, trying hard to figure out what the bee meant; he then slowly shook it from side to side to indicate he still had no idea what Bastian was talking about. "Sorry, Bastian, but I don't get it."

"Don't worry. It isn't important," she told him. "I was just trying to be funny. I've heard different creatures have different funny bones, and I guess a bee's humour isn't the same as it is for a dog. Not everything you hear is worth trying to understand, you know."

"I see. I guess that means I should pick my lessons carefully," Smudge replied with a quick wag of his tail. He stood up to give his body another well-needed stretch. As he did, he glanced up and noticed the sun had almost reached the middle of the sky. The day was still pleasantly warm and he suggested they continue down the driveway. Together they wandered along with Bastian droning comfortably in the dog's ear as she flew above his head. Smudge stopped several times to sniff at bushes, flowers, rocks and various clumps of grass along the way. He even ran his nose over the warm cement a few times to catch new scents, but eventually his muzzle lead him back to the tall grasses beside the pavement, where Bastian was exploring the few remaining wildflowers. She finally chose one and landed on the smooth petals. Smudge found a comfortable spot in the dry grass beside her and sat back down.

"So, what else can we learn from your C lessons?" he asked.

"Oh, it has so many good things to teach us," the bee hummed, delighted to be asked to share her knowledge. "My favourite has four different points to think about. Do you want to hear it?"

"Sure. *It's a good day if you learn something new,*" the dog cheerily echoed what the bee had said earlier.

"Okay. The first point is that can't and can are opposites attached to each other by change." The bee left the flower and flew in a straight line in front of the dog as if to draw an imaginary line in the air.

Smudge pretended he could see the words in the air with change in the middle and can't and can at either end.

Can't - - - - - - - -change- - - - - - - - Can

Bastian demonstrated the next two points by flying first to one end of the line and then back to the other saying: "The only way to move from can't to can is to change direction."

Can't - - - - - - - -change- - - - - - - - Can

"And the only way to move from can to can't is to...change direction."

Can't - - - - - - - -change- - - - - - - - Can

Smudge nodded. So far it made sense to him. "What's the fourth point, Bastian?"

"The fourth point is about courage, because change isn't really possible without it."

On hearing this, Smudge imagined the word courage hanging down from the centre of his imaginary line.

```
                    C
                    O
Can't .....change U change....... Can
                    R
                    A
                    G
                    E
```

"I think courage must be the most important part since it separates can't from can," Smudge said, feeling quite proud of how well he was understanding this lesson.

"Might be," Bastian hummed.

"But Bastian, is it really possible to change ourselves? I mean, I'm a dog and can't be anything but a dog, right?"

"Hmmm, good question. I've heard that a truly wise creature understands what it can change and what it can't. I don't know if it's possible to change what we are. I think I'll always be a bee. However, I do know we can change how we act. If we don't like the direction we're flying, we can always decide to turn and fly the other way."

"Or walk or run, since dogs can't fly," Smudge added. He made a valiant effort to flap his ears up and down, but went nowhere, proving his point. "I guess it would help us understand others if we could figure out which way they're flying and why they're going that way."

Bastian nodded in agreement. "One thing I know for sure is that a bee can't fly in every direction at once."

"I guess you'd pull yourself apart," the dog woofed in laughter. "Well, you were right about lesson C. I've learned some good things, especially about courage. It means being afraid of something, but doing it anyway, like turning around and going back when you've run away from something really hard." He sighed; "but I'm not sure if understanding it will make it any easier."

"It helps," Bastian replied, and began to hum softly.

"Why you're even smarter than I thought you were, little dog," interrupted a rumbling voice from behind them, making the dog jump.

They turned to see a huge, brown bear towering over them, his hairy coat looking thoroughly rumpled, as if he'd just spent a glorious morning rolling about in a big field of clover. He'd approached so quietly that neither dog nor bee had noticed him until he had spoken. Smudge recognized him as the bear from the day before and smiled a hello, but Bastian wasn't quite so friendly. She began to buzz very loudly and flew toward the creature, darting back and forth above his shaggy head in a way that made it plain she was quite upset. The bear backed up several feet, cowering down in the grass and covering his eyes with two giant, clawed paws. Smudge immediately realized that the bear was afraid and desperately trying to make himself invisible. It didn't work.

"Wait!" the bear pleaded with the angry bee. "I just came to listen to the little dog! I learned a few things from him yesterday and thought I'd come back to hear more!"

"You're just a thief!" bristled the bee, her stinger shining in the noonday sun.

On seeing this, Smudge hurried over to try and rescue the bear from the tiny bee's fury. "Bastian, at least give him a chance to apologize if he took something he shouldn't," he pleaded.

The bee buzzed a little less loudly, though she remained hovering over the cowering bear.

"Well?" she snapped at him.

"I'm not trying to steal anything from you," he replied. "Honestly."

"But you've tried to steal my hive's honey in the past," she buzzed a little louder.

"I won't ever do it again," promised the bear in a frightened voice. "I just got really hungry and the smell of honey was so delicious. Honey's the best food in the world, after all."

The bee's buzzing softened with this compliment and her face took on a less angry look, although it was still quite stern. It reminded Smudge of a parent he'd once seen who'd had to scold a child for taking a cookie they knew wasn't theirs. The huge bear threw a pleading look toward the tiny bee and her barbed stinger, as if asking for mercy. Smudge moved closer to the creature and whispered an encouraging word for him to be brave.

"I really am sorry," the bear continued, seeming to relax a little. "I wasn't trying to hurt the bees. It's just hard not to take something you want so much."

"If you take our honey, what will we eat during the cold winter months?" she demanded.

"I never thought of that," the bear admitted. "I guess I was only thinking of myself and what I wanted." He looked very sad, and added, "It would be kind of like bees loving nectar and then being told by the flowers not to take any."

The moment she heard this Bastian's buzzing stopped completely. Smudge wondered if it was because the bee had just learned a new perspective.

"I understand how you feel," she hummed. "The difference is that the flowers want us to take the nectar. We don't steal it from them without asking."

"Yeah," the bear mumbled, shaking his head. "This little dog explained some of that to me yesterday."

"What did Smudge say?" Bastian asked in curiosity.

The bear gave a lopsided grin. "Why, he told me about how making bee friends might give me a chance to share some of their honey without getting stung."

"He did?" The bee buzzed over to Smudge and sat on his nose, so she could better look into his eyes.

Smudge nodded nervously, unsure if Bastian was mad at him. The sudden movement caused her to lose balance and fall from her perch. A quick flip in the air and she was back upright and flying around them.

"Well, the more I live, the more I learn," she said with a sudden laugh. "Okay bear, you're welcome to a small portion of honey from our hive if you're willing to do some hard work for it."

"Really? Thank you!" the bear replied enthusiastically. This outburst was followed by a pause and he continued on in a more cautious voice. "Umm...what would you want me to do?"

"Why, keep other bears from stealing our honey, of course!" came her prompt reply.

"What? That's all?" The bear was all smiles again. "Consider it done!" he bellowed.

"You'd really help us?" Bastian asked in astonishment.

"Sure, why not?" the bear rumbled.

"What will the other bears think of you?" asked Smudge.

"Oh, they won't mind. I'm bigger than them," the brown bear chuckled.

"Some creatures don't give a hoot about what others think of them," Bastian stated.

"Yeah. Some don't. It's a good way to end up being alone, though," replied the bear with a sudden sigh. He sat back on his haunches as if trying to decide whether to say anything more.

The three creatures stared at each other in silence until finally the bear gave a great huff and stood up again.

"Up until yesterday, I didn't care much about what others thought of me," he boomed. "I never got along well with other bears and I'd just whack anything out of my way that I didn't like, unless it was bigger than me." The bear looked at Smudge with a sorry expression, as if regretting what he'd almost done when the little dog had first come barking at him.

Smudge forgave him with a friendly wag of his tail. "It must have been hard for you to not get mad at me for barking like that. I'm sure glad you took the time to talk to me instead."

"Well, I figured I sort of owed you since you were kind enough to leave out your garbage for me," admitted the bear.

"Oh, that wasn't me, it was my master. But he says you should never eat garbage food because it isn't good for you."

"He's talking about the human who lives with him," Bastian explained to the bear.

"I like garbage food," muttered the bear.

"Well, he told me bears are better off to eat food from the forest. He said bears are smart and learn really fast when it comes to finding food."

"He did? Why, what a nice thing to say," beamed the bear. "I didn't realize humans could be so kind."

"Humans do have some very good points," Bastian spoke up.

"Food is one of my favourite things," the bear confided to them, "so I do learn about it really fast. I don't learn anything else fast, though."

"Learning our lessons fast may not be as important as learning them well," Bastian called down from her position high above their heads.

Smudge quickly told the bear about the bee's lessons, a dog's important words and what he and Bastian had learned from sharing with each other.

"I guess you're both pretty smart then," the bear said with another great sigh. "I'm pretty slow. Even the other bears say so."

"Me too," Smudge consoled. "I had to take a training class with my master when I was a puppy and boy did he get mad at me a few times. It took me forever to learn what 'stay' meant."

Bastian flew back down to the same level as the other two, landing on a nearby log. "I wasn't always good at learning either," she admitted to them. "I was only a C student, and it took me a long time to learn my lessons. When I finally did, I got so excited I just couldn't wait to share them!"

With those words she launched back off the log, flying in circles that became bigger and bigger, as if to show her delight in what she had learned.

"I guess being slow isn't such a bad thing," concluded Smudge.

"I don't think you're slow," growled the bear.

"Me neither," Bastian chimed in. "Maybe it was your human who just didn't understand the lesson he was supposed to be learning."

"You mean he was supposed to learn to stay too?" asked the bear in confusion.

"No, I don't mean that," Bastian bristled a bit impatiently. "I mean sometimes, when someone, like a teacher or a master, or even a mama bear, wants us to learn a lesson, they're supposed to learn something too."

"And what they're trying to teach us...and what we actually learn from them...can be very different things." The bear spoke slowly, as if not used to sharing his thoughts.

Bastian looked surprised by the bear's words, as though she hadn't expected a smart comment from such a slow-thinking creature.

"Gee, I wonder what my master was supposed to be learning?" mused Smudge.

"Probably patience," Bastian suggested.

"Oh...I get it," said Smudge, "but I'm not so sure he'll ever learn that lesson."

"Not unless he wants to, and even then it's hard to get it right all the time," said Bastian. "I still get impatient sometimes, even though I try not to." She gave the bear an apologetic look. "Every bee knows you can't learn to spell unless you're willing to work at your spelling lessons. Smudge, you wouldn't have learned to stay if you hadn't wanted to."

"I guess that's true. Maybe I need to work harder on patience too." Smudge grinned. "Patience and doggedness when it comes to my master."

The bear looked confused again, so Smudge patiently explained that doggedness meant the same as perseverance or not giving up. At first the bear struggled with this idea, but Smudge was persistent in his explanations until the bear understood.

Bastian beamed at Smudge. "You're quite a good teacher," she praised him.

"Thanks, Bastian. Practise makes perfect, as my master often says."

"Too true," she replied. "That's probably why you're so good at understanding what humans say. Most other creatures I've spoken with find them quite hard to understand. Sometimes they seem so smart, yet at other times not so smart."

"I have to agree with the bee, little dog," grunted the bear. "It's awfully nice of your human to say my kind are smart, but I've run into some humans who are very slow learners. For instance, if they don't want me to eat their garbage, why do they keep putting it out night after night?" He gave a great, booming laugh and raised a paw to scratch a thick patch of fur at the back of his head.

As Smudge watched the bear, a less pleasant thought occurred to him. Being more familiar with the habits of humans, he decided to warn his new companion about the potential danger of misjudging them.

"You'd best be careful, bear. Some humans set traps. What if they just keep putting out their garbage to lure you back so they can sting you with their guns?"

The bear stopped laughing, looking both startled and frightened. Obviously the idea that a human might outsmart a bear had never occurred to him before. "I guess I don't understand as much as I thought," he rumbled, sitting down with a great huff. "I guess I'm as stupid as the other bears say."

"You aren't stupid!" Smudge barked, jumping to the bear's defence. "Nobody knows everything. That's why we need each other. So we can share stuff and all get smarter. You shouldn't be afraid to ask for help."

"I wish I was brave enough to ask for help," squeaked a small, timid voice from behind a nearby rock.

Dog, bee and bear turned toward the spot from where the voice had come. A chipmunk's head popped into view, and was met by three pairs of staring eyes. The small creature instantly disappeared again. After a moment, two small ears rose above the rock, followed by two small eyes. Once again they met the stares of Smudge, Bastian and the bear, and once again they vanished from sight.

"I wish I could disappear that easily," murmured the bear to no one in particular.

Smudge nodded. He'd been thinking the same thing, and realized the chipmunk probably wasn't going to come out without being coaxed. "It's okay, Jester. We won't hurt you," he called gently.

Slowly the small chipmunk came back into view. He shivered

as he worked his way around the rock, his small, striped back pressed against its hard surface as if it might stop him from disappearing again. With a careful bow toward the three others, he glanced nervously about for anything else that might harm him. Seeing nothing, he took a deep breath, as if to speak, then stopped. Instead he grabbed his tail and ran his small paws up and down its bushy length in a worried sort of way.

"Jester, did you say something about asking for help?" Smudge tired coaxing him again.

"Y-yes," the chipmunk squeaked in fear. "That is, I found those c-carrots you left and...and w-wanted to thank you." The words came out in a series of stuttering bursts and terrified gulps, as if the small creature were afraid even his words of thanks might cause the dog to bark and give chase.

"You're welcome," Smudge said as kindly as he knew how. "I'm glad you found them okay. They're from the garden my master planted."

"He's talking about his human," the bear explained.

"Oh? Should I th-thank him too?" the chipmunk asked anxiously.

"Probably not right now," Smudge advised him. "But I'll do my best to let him know for you. He gives me carrots in return for guarding our garden, and I thought if I shared some with you and your family you might agree to leave the garden alone."

The chipmunk looked baffled. "G-guarding the g-garden? I don't know what that means," he stuttered in nervousness.

"Guarding is my job," Smudge patiently explained in an effort to get the smaller creature to relax. "That's why I have to chase you away when you steal from us. In return for keeping our garden safe, my master shares his food with me. He's the one who does the hard work of planting seeds, pulling weeds and watering the earth when the sky won't send rain."

"Oh dear! I didn't know the garden belonged to anyone!" gasped the chipmunk. "I thought carrots just g-grew in places like that, the same as honey grows on trees."

These words caused an instant reaction from Bastian, who began buzzing loudly in the background. The chipmunk continued, quite unaware of the bee's agitation.

"I thought you chased me because you were m-mean." He said these last words in a frightened whisper.

"Mean? Me? I'm not mean!" Smudge barked, looking quite hurt.

He turned away from the smaller creature and gave a great sniff. The chipmunk looked on in surprise, his small eyes becoming as big as saucers. When the dog gave a second sniff the chipmunk cautiously moved toward him, timidly placing a small paw on Smudge's black and white fur.

"I see now how wrong I've been about you. You're very generous to share with us. I'll find some way to repay you." The chipmunk patted Smudge as if consoling a youngster.

Smudge's tail gave a slow wag to show he was listening.

"I'll make sure none of my family takes anything from your garden again," the chipmunk hurried on. "We'll just gather what we need from other places and check to make sure it doesn't belong to you."

"Good idea," buzzed Bastian, landing gracefully on a blade of grass in front of the small chipmunk. "Especially since honey is made by hard-working bees and certainly doesn't just grow on trees!"

Jester jumped back and Bastian turned toward the bear to make sure he too was listening. The shaggy, brown creature responded by hanging his huge head and covering his eyes with both paws, trying once again to make himself invisible. It didn't work.

"Thanks, Jester," Smudge spoke up, giving his wet nose a swipe. "It was Bastian who gave me the idea of sharing."

The chipmunk bobbed his head up and down toward the bee, saying in a quick flurry of gratitude: "I heard you talking earlier. It's good of you to share what you know."

"My pleasure," Bastian droned. "And perhaps you can repay Smudge's kindness by telling those pesky mice and rabbits about who does all the hard work to make those vegetables grow; then he won't have as much guarding to do."

"Oh, I'll gladly do that! And maybe Smudge can teach us how to grow our own carrots!" exclaimed Jester, quite beside himself with excitement. He rushed back and forth between Smudge and Bastian, thanking each for all they'd shared, even stopping at the bear once to thank him too.

This greatly puzzled the huge creature. "Whatever are you thanking me for?" he asked in astonishment.

"Just for listening!" squeaked the chipmunk.

"Umm, well, I'm happy to oblige," the bear answered. "Ah...let me know if there's anything else I can do." He said it with a doubtful look.

"Well..." the chipmunk hesitated, becoming nervous again and moving his eyes from one creature to another, "I'm sorry for having listened earlier without asking, but, well...would you mind if I stayed and listened a bit longer? I really need to learn how to be braver." His small body trembled as he waited for their answer.

"Sure you can stay, but having the courage to come and talk with us makes me think you're already quite brave," Smudge told him.

"Me?" gulped the chipmunk. "No! Not at all!"

"I think you're wrong," said Bastian. "Maybe you just need

to understand yourself better."

"Yeah. It takes courage to admit you aren't good at something, and even more to ask for help, and you've done both," the bear pointed out.

Jester turned to face the brown bear, his smaller body quaking in fear before such a huge animal. "What should we do if we find the courage to ask for help, but whoever we ask hurts us instead of helping us?"

"Hmmm....That's a tough one." The bear paused to rub the top of his head, as if that might help him think of an answer. It seemed to work. He grunted and said, "Got it. We just back up from them and keep searching until we find someone willing to help."

"And what if they want to help us, but we ask too many questions because we don't understand easily, and they just get tired and end up biting us?" the chipmunk persisted in his fast flurry of words.

"You mean, what if we're just too slow for them?" the bear asked.

Jester gave a nervous nod.

"Only they can decide to be patient enough to help," Smudge pointed out.

"And we have to decide if we're willing to understand them back," Bastian added.

"You know what they say, we have to trust that others will give us what we need so we can give them what they want," the chipmunk chattered.

"Sounds a bit nutty to me," rumbled the bear under his breath.

"I don't know about that," Smudge said slowly. "I think it

does kind of make sense. It's like two creatures who don't speak the same language. If one wants help and the other is willing to give it, they still need to learn each other's language before they can get anywhere."

"Oh," said the bear, scratching his head. "Ohhhhhhh...." he repeated again in a long drawn out way, as if suddenly he truly understood. "So, if I'm the one who wants help, I'd need to ask others to explain things over and over again because I sort of forget after awhile."

"That's it," the chipmunk timidly confirmed. "And since I asked for your help, if it isn't too much trouble, that is, and you don't mind too much, then you need to know I learn stuff best in small bits."

"Those are exactly the kinds of thing we need to know," Bastian buzzed happily. "And, of course, you already know how I like to move about when I speak." She did a few loops in the air to stress her point. "It helps me think things through, but since I know it's easier for some of you if I don't fly around too much, I'll try and give you what you need, hoping you'll be kind enough to give me what I want most."

"What's that?" Jester asked with a nervous twitch of his tail.

"Why, to learn as much as I can!" grinned the bee. "And the best way to make that happen is to listen to others and try to see things through their eyes."

"I'd be satisfied if I could just figure out who wants short answers and who wants long ones," Smudge groaned. "It seems some creatures need next to nothing to understand and others need almost everything; but who knows which is which until we ask or they tell?" Smudge watched his tiny bee friend doing figure eights in the air and noted her pleased smile. She certainly seemed at her happiest when figuring something out or learning something new.

Bastian completed another loop, then flew down to perch on

the dog's nose. "No one," she replied to his question. "And we'll never get to know each other well if we let that happen."

"Don't forget how willing I was to sit on your nose to see things through your eyes," Smudge jokingly reminded her.

"Ah, but I wasn't willing to let you, was I?" she teased back. "It would have hurt me too much."

"I can certainly see your point of view," the little dog laughed.

The bear remained sitting on his haunches during this exchange, continuing to scratch here and there. His face bore a rather thoughtful expression.

"Hey, Bastian," he called to her, "remember that thing you said about Jester needing to understand himself?"

She nodded.

"Well, I've been thinking about it, and I've started to wonder if others might be running away from me because they're afraid."

"Of course it's why we run!" squealed Jester, jumping up and down in a great fluster.

"Humph! If they'd just stop barking and running they'd soon know I wouldn't hurt a fly—well, not much anyway," the bear said.

"What do you mean by 'not much'? Those are the exact kind of words that make others want to fly away," Bastian scolded him. She flew off, making a bee-line for the top of the fir tree.

The bear looked so hurt at her sudden departure that the tiny bee relented and flew back down, hovering above his dark snout.

"I don't mean to hurt anyone," he mumbled, lowering his huge head. "I can't help it if other creatures are afraid of me just because I growl sometimes."

"Can't you?" Smudge asked.

The bear's eyes moved toward the little dog as if sizing him up. This was followed by a heavy sigh. "I suppose I *could* try to stop growling so much," he admitted.

"Being willing to try is the most important part," Smudge encouraged him.

"I agree," Bastian hummed gently, "and it's also important to know that sometimes others move away because they're afraid they might hurt us back."

Her soft words caused the bear to raise his snout and Bastian promptly landed on his wide, moist nose. He didn't swat at her and she was very careful to keep her stinger out of the way. The pair stared at each other for several moments, and it was plain to see that neither wanted to hurt the other.

"At least you're able to move away from me if you want to," the bear finally muttered, shaking his head from side to side. "Sometimes I wish I could run away from myself."

Bastian hurriedly beat her wings in an effort to keep her balance. Once her footing had been regained, she droned, "I'll bet it's not easy being a bear."

"Probably no harder than being a bee," the bear replied with a crooked smile.

Smudge looked at the odd pair in admiration. "I wish we could know things like that without having to figure them out the hard way," he said.

Bastian threw him a smile, and her tiny wings began to flutter. In a moment she was airborne.

THE OTHER SIDE OF ME

"They say we learn things better the hard way," Jester informed them, chewing nervously on a small paw.

"Whoever said such a silly thing can't have had much to learn," grunted the bear.

"Or else didn't learn what they were taught when they should have, and so had to find out the hard way," Smudge suggested. He was remembering the time he'd disobeyed his master and gone too close to the fireplace. He'd certainly learned the hard way that time and had spent a week licking his poor, burnt paw trying to make the pain go away.

"Humph. I suppose so," grumbled the bear, who preferred things to be easy. "Wouldn't it be simpler if we could just see how we look to others so we could figure out how to do things better?"

The idea quite struck Smudge and he tilted his head to one side, as he often did when trying to figure something out. "I never thought about it before, but now you have me wondering," he told the bear. "I wonder what it's like to be on the other side of me?"

"I can tell you," whispered Jester, shaking like a small, brown leaf. "When you bark, it's scary, and all I can think to do is run away and hide."

"Sorry," Smudge apologized. "I won't do it anymore. But, Jester, I'm curious about something. I've noticed that sometimes you hesitate and don't run right away. Why is that?"

"It's because of my family. If they're about I wait until they're safe before I run to save myself," the chipmunk explained with a shiver.

"Being willing to help someone else, when your afraid for

yourself, is the bravest thing of all," Bastian solemnly informed him.

Smudge and the bear nodded in agreement. Jester looked surprised and pleased to hear this, and suddenly stood a little taller and prouder. It seemed he was getting quite a different picture of himself when seen through others' eyes.

"Well, when I hear barking it makes me want to swat real hard," admitted the bear. "I find that usually quietens noisy creatures."

"Sometimes permanently," murmured the bee.

"I heard that," grumped the bear. "But I suppose you're right. Doesn't give me much of a chance to get to know them if I'm swinging at them. I guess I should wait until they stop and then maybe we can get somewhere. Anyway, most creatures don't bother barking at me. They usually just run away as fast as they can. Makes me mad that they won't stay and give me a chance."

"I bet if you gave them a chance first they might be willing to give you one too," Bastian suggested.

"I could try, although I'd have to work really hard to not get mad," the bear replied. "I think it might be a bit easier now that I know what you get in return for trying."

"What's that?" asked Smudge.

"Friends," the bear grunted. He gave the dog a playful swat, being extra careful not to let his huge claws touch the little dog.

"Well, I know how you feel," Bastian confided. "Being on the other side of me can be scary, I suppose, at least to those who only see my stinger and nothing else."

"It's because we don't know if you'll use it or not," the bear replied. "When we see a weapon like you have, it doesn't matter how tiny you are, it's scary."

"I see your point, but we can't just make our stingers disappear. I think I'd rather others just ran away from us like they do you," she told the bear. "Instead they usually swat first then wonder why they get stung."

"So what should we do if we meet a strange bee that's buzzing too close and making us afraid?" the chipmunk asked.

"Just stay still. We need to study you to see if you're a flower. Once you understand what we're doing it won't seem scary anymore. Most bees are good and won't hurt you unless you frighten them. I can't promise you'll never get stung by another bee, but I can promise you it's worth giving us a chance. I think it's the kind of chance you want too, bear."

The huge, brown bear gave a solemn nod of agreement.

"It's probably not that others don't want to give you a chance," the chipmunk suddenly piped up, "but just imagine what it's like to be small, without a stinger or a big, barking voice. Imagine you don't have huge, clawed paws to defend yourself. You might find out the hard way why it's safer to run away from creatures like you." He backed up a bit, as though afraid his words might have made them angry, and only stopped when he reached a large rock.

Smudge wondered if having something solid at his back made the chipmunk feel more secure. The dog wagged his tail to encourage the chipmunk to keep talking, and since no one else looked upset the small creature seemed to find his courage once again.

"When I was young I felt really safe with my family," he began to explain. "There were twelve of us living together, and we younger ones played most of the day. We weren't very wise, though. Being surrounded by kindness, we thought all creatures would want to be our friends. The rabbits were nice enough to us, and so were the mice and squirrels. Oh, sometimes we'd argue over a seed or nut, but mostly we got along quite well. Then my uncle met a cat and didn't come home again. One of my brothers ran into a big snake and it was the last we saw of him. A hawk took my youngest sister. We learned the hard way that just because we wanted to be friends didn't mean others felt the same way. By the time I started my own family there were only three of us left. I've made sure to teach my youngsters that the world isn't always a friendly place; it can hurt you if you don't learn to run and hide." A small tear slid from the chipmunk's eye and he hurriedly wiped it away, as if he didn't want to look weaker than he was.

Smudge felt tears sting his own eyes, and wasn't at all surprised to see the bear and bee having the same problem. "Do you think it's possible that all creatures might learn to be friends some day?" he asked them.

"I don't know," grunted the bear in a gruff voice. "I think we'd all need to try a little harder to understand what it's like to be on the other side of us before that could happen."

"If we start taking the time to figure out why others sting, swat, bark or run away from us, and are willing to work on fixing ourselves, we might eventually be able to live together as friends instead of enemies," said Bastian solemnly.

"Jester, how did you ever find the courage to come and talk to us today?" Smudge asked in awe. "After all the bad things that have happened in your family, no one could blame you if you decided to stay hidden away."

"For awhile I did just that," the chipmunk admitted in a low voice. "I was so afraid I couldn't make myself step outside of our den. After a bit I came to realize I was trapped there by my own fear and was hurting myself more than the things I was afraid of; so I made up my mind to go out, even if it meant getting hurt." He stopped to clear his throat and began again in a calmer voice. "I was scared, but it felt great to be outside again, and in time my fear grew less. It's not gone, but every morning I remind myself that the only way to overcome fear is to go out and face whatever scares me." The chipmunk rose up on his back legs as he said this, looking more fierce than the others would have thought possible for such a small, defenceless creature.

"Wow," Smudge woofed in admiration. "Kind of like arguing yourself out of being afraid."

"Sort of," Jester replied, dropping his front paws back onto the sun-warmed grass. "And the more often I do it, the less I seem to worry."

"Well, now you know us and can see you had even less to worry about than you thought," Smudge pointed out.

"Hold on a minute. I don't think it's that simple," the bear cut in. "It's true we're all getting along because we've gotten to know each other better, but what about cows?"

"Huh?" the other three asked in confusion.

"You heard me. Cows," the bear repeated with a snort. "I've never eaten one, but I've heard they taste great. So how do you suppose someone who eats cows could possibly become friends with them? hey wouldn't be able to think of anything except supper!"

Jester turned rather pale at these words and Smudge suddenly seemed very interested in one of his paws, lifting it up and turning it over to look at both sides. Still staring intently at his toenails he cleared his throat to get their attention.

"Ahem. Er...umm...well, you all know humans take care of cows and eat them too, right?" When the others nodded in response, the dog lowered his head and muttered, "Well...I've had a few bites myself and they tasted awfully good."

"There!I knew it!" shrieked the chipmunk, his small body pressed once more against a rock. "How can we be friends with someone who's willing to eat another creature!"

"Oh, calm down Jester!" the bear growled at him

impatiently. "Humans eat cows because they need food. Does it upset you that I've eaten salmon? They're delicious, and it's just part of what bears eat, the same as chipmunks eat nuts and seeds."

"And bird's eggs," Smudge barked rather defensively. "My master says chipmunks are known to raid nests from time to time. I don't see how that's any different."

Jester's fur seemed to grow even paler, and it was his turn to lower his head and exam his paws.

"Yeah, so calm down and keep your fur on," the bear told him. "We're friends now, we're not going to hurt you and I promise no one else will either while I'm around."

The chipmunk looked up with an expression that changed from fear to relief so quickly it almost made Smudge laugh.

"Oh. I'd forgotten for a moment that we're friends. Would you really protect me?" Jester asked doubtfully.

"I said I would, didn't I? And I bet Smudge and Bastian would too," the bear added with a throaty huff.

The bee quickly nodded her agreement and Smudge wagged his tail.

"Of course I would!" he woofed. "My master says we should always protect the underdog."

"The what?" Jester asked with a puzzled look.

"He means the smallest dog; the weakest one who needs help from bigger, stronger dogs," Bastian explained to the chipmunk.

"Hey, Smudge, that human of yours sounds like a pretty good sort. I should come by sometime to meet him," offered the bear.

"I don't think he's quite ready for you yet," Smudge quickly replied. The thought of introducing his master to the huge bear gave him a strange feeling inside, like bees buzzing in his stomach.

"Oh, okay. Just let me know when," the bear replied good-naturedly. "And hey, Jester, I understand why the thing about cows upsets you," he continued. "But what if you suddenly found out bird's eggs had feelings? Would you still eat them?"

The chipmunk had calmed back down and had let go of the rock to come forward and rejoin the group. He paused for a moment to think about this interesting question. "I don't know," he finally admitted. "I never thought about it before."

"Well, you should try to understand that cows are just as much food to some of us as bird's eggs are to others," the bear suggested; "and, while I never thought about it from a cow's point of view before, now that I am, maybe I need to consider how they might feel." He raised himself to full his height to take a stretch, and then gave a great sigh and plopped back down on all fours. It was done with the air of someone about to give up a long-desired treat. "I guess I could say no to ever eating cows if it meant that much to them," he said with great effort. "I suppose I could even try being friends with them; however, I absolutely refuse to lay around all day chewing grass! What a waste of time when there's so many better things to do."

"What about salmon?" Bastian asked in curiosity.

"What about them?" the bear began to ask, then stopped with a gasp of dismay. "You can't mean I have to be friends with them too?" He looked horrified at the thought.

"Well, if you talk to them instead of eating them you might learn a few new things that you could share with us," coaxed the bee.

The bear wore a very unhappy expression and pawed repeatedly at the ground.

"You'd still have some of my honey after all," Bastian added.

"I'll think about it," growled the bear, turning to look in the other direction.

Smudge felt sorry for him. Perhaps Bastian was asking the bear to give up too much all at once. The dog was beginning to realize how hard it must be to give up something you really liked, even when you knew it was the right thing to do. No matter how much you might want to understand someone else's perspective, you were still going to need time to get used to new ideas. Being patient with yourself seemed an important thing too. He told his friends what he was thinking.

"Thank you for sharing and for all you've taught me today," squeaked the chipmunk in reply, standing up as if ready to leave. "I'm starting to understand things much better now."

"Wait! I haven't taught you a single lesson," protested Bastian, moving to a spot in front of the chipmunk, as if to prevent him from leaving before she had a chance to have her say.

"Oh, but you have," Jester replied firmly. "I used to think it best to run from a growling bear, a barking dog and a stinging bee. You've shown me that learning more about what scares me is the first step to overcoming fear. It may not change what I'm afraid of, but it sure changes how I'll look at it, and that's bound to make a difference."

"I think it's our nature to see what scares us first and to want to move away, instead of seeing the reward we might gain by moving closer. That's why some creatures may never look past my stinger to find out that I'm a nice bee," Bastian sighed.

The chipmunk nodded and carefully patted the tiny bee on the head, almost knocking her over. "That's sad, but I think you're right, Bastian. From now on I'm going to teach my family to learn as much as they can about whatever they're afraid of and then I'll encourage them to move forward, as long as they aren't hurting themselves or others."

"Even though there's a chance something bad could happen?" questioned Bastian.

"I think so," the chipmunk slowly replied, "because there's also the chance it will lead to a good consequence, like new friends."

BEAR ESSENTIALS

"So now that you have me, Bastian and this bear to look out for you, you won't have to—" Smudge began to say to the chipmunk, but stopped himself mid-sentence to turn and look back at the huge bear. "Wait a minute, what's your name?"

The bear responded by rolling over onto the thick, yellow stalks of grass and thrashing about, sending up a cloud of dust that blew over his companions. By the time he rolled back onto his stomach, his fur was littered with bits of dried grass.

"What's your name?" Smudge repeated, thinking the bear hadn't heard him.

The shaggy creature shuffled from one paw to the other, looking as though he'd rather not tell them.

"Oh come on, how bad can it be?" queried Bastian.

"Don't you have a name?" the chipmunk gently asked.

"Barely," the huge monster finally admitted, looking embarrassed.

"You barely have a name?" Smudge questioned, looking as confused as the others.

"No," growled the brown bear impatiently, "that is my name. Barely. Mama and Papa bear thought me so tiny when I was born they said I was barely there."

"You? Tiny?" the others all questioned at once.

"It was their bear humour," muttered the brown bear. "For a bear cub I was pretty small."

"I see," Bastian hummed with a smile.

"I think you've outgrown your name," added Jester.

The others couldn't help laughing out loud at this comment, and Barely joined in.

"I guess I have," he admitted, "but Mama and Papa bear thought it was a good name for me. They used to tell me stories of Barely the Brave, one of the most famous bears in bear history. He was a small bear who went out into the world and had all sorts of big adventures. He liked to help other bears in need, but often barely got away in time to save his own skin."

"He sounds like a very good bear if he was willing to help others. What happened to him?" Bastian asked in curiosity.

"Oh, he finally figured out courage didn't mean going out and risking your skin just to prove yourself and sort of changed his direction in life."

Bastian nodded, as if to say she knew exactly what the bear meant.

"He decided that, if you must have adventures and aren't content to stay in your den, you can at least stick closer to the forest and farther away from humans," Barely continued. "That was before humans moved into the forest, of course. Anyway, he spent the rest of his life sharing his stories with younger bears to help them avoid some of the dangers he'd come across in his travels so they wouldn't fall into the same snares."

"Now there's a bear I wish I'd met," sighed Bastian.

"Yeah. Some of the stories about him were really good," said Barely, "especially the one where he fell into a giant pit and spent days trying to get out. He'd almost given up hope when a bird came along—one that he'd once been kind to. She flew down to tell him to stop his jumping and climbing and just start digging. From the sky she could see the pit had been dug near the edge of a low cliff that fell into a ravine. The bear started to dig on the side of the pit the bird showed him and in no time he broke free and tumbled down into the ravine."

"Was he hurt?" the chipmunk asked in a worried voice.

"Nope, just dirty. Fortunately there was a creek at the bottom so he could wash up. Mama bear used to say the most important part of that story was to remember to wash your paws after digging in the dirt, but Papa bear thought it said more about how the bear's kindness to a bird saved his own life in the end."

"I think you're papa bear was right," breathed Jester.

"So Barely the Brave thought jumping and climbing was the way out of the pit, but it took a bird's eye view to show him a different way out," Bastian buzzed.

"Proving that there's more than one way to skin a cat," laughed Smudge.

Three pairs of eyes locked onto the dog in shocked surprise.

"Pardon?" Jester whispered.

"Oh, it's just something my master says. It's supposed to be a funny way of saying how there's more than one way to do things," explained the dog, feeling a bit uncomfortable.

No one smiled.

"It's sort of a joke," he muttered.

No one laughed.

"I guess you're right about funny bones, Bastian. It depends on the creature," he finished lamely.

"A joke isn't funny if it hurts someone," the chipmunk stated in a serious voice. "I don't have any cat friends, but I've heard that some humans skin small animals to get their fur."

"Big ones too," growled Barely. "Apparently bears make nice rugs!" He grimaced and rose to his full, towering height. For a moment he looked so fierce that the others all wanted to run away. However, he quickly dropped back down to the ground. "It was one of the first bear essentials Mama and Papa bear taught me when I was a cub," he continued. "That, and how to tell the difference between too hot, too cold and just right."

"What are bear essentials?" Smudge asked, hoping to change the subject. Although he hadn't meant to hurt anyone with his words, the little dog was feeling rather badly about what he'd said. Jester no longer looked upset with him, but Smudge could still feel the huge bear gazing at him and reluctantly met his eyes. With relief he noted Barely had relaxed and no longer looked offended.

"They're kind of like Bastian's lessons and your important words," Barely grunted.

"Ah, things a bear needs to know," Bastian nodded wisely.

"Yeah. Most of them were too hard to learn, so I didn't pay much attention. Papa bear did his best to teach me and boy did Mama bear growl when I didn't listen...which was most of the time," Barely chuckled. "I barely remember any of them now."

 # F AND G

"Maybe it's time to learn knew things," the chipmunk suggested timidly.

"Good idea, Jester," Smudge said approvingly. "Hey, Bastian, what's that thing you were humming earlier about your lessons from the hive?"

"Ah! Bee lessons!" she said excitedly. "Ahem."

She cleared her throat and began to recite in a sweet voice.

> *"Lessons usually come in three's*
> *At least according to the bees"*

She'd hardly begun when Smudge interrupted.

"Whoa there, Bastian. Lesson C had way more than three!" he reminded her.

"True. But the more you listen, the more you'll learn," she scolded, flying in circles above him. Smudge settled back down with a nod, and once again Bastian began her happy humming.

> *"But lesson F and lesson G*
> *Have two and one, and then there's C*
> *It has numerous things to show*
> *Should we decide we want to grow"*

They listened to her words and watched in fascination as she twirled and danced in the soft wind that had just begun to blow. Finishing off her beautiful, aerial ballet with a low bow, she flew to an old tree stump and landed on the weather-beaten, sun-faded wood. "Sooner or later most of us choose to grow, although sadly some just won't," she told them, folding back her wings.

"There'll always be those who refuse to grow in the right direction," Barely agreed.

"It's never always," Smudge cut in. "Never always and never never, so my master tells me."

"Well, you know what they say—there's an exception to every rule!" shrilled the chipmunk as he jumped onto the same stump where Bastian perched.

"They say, they say—you keep saying that, but who are they anyway?" Smudge barked, feeling a bit impatient with the smaller creature, and not recognizing how often he did the same sort of thing himself when he repeated what his master said.

"Many of us say *'they say'* from time to time—" Bastian began to drone, but was interrupted in turn by Jester.

"It's okay, Bastian, I can answer. *'They'* are those who tell, teach or tattle," Jester squeaked. "The bigger the family that comes together, the more of *them* there are."

"Oh...well that makes sense," Smudge admitted in an apologetic tone.

"Not to me it doesn't," boomed Barely, sitting back on his haunches.

"I'll try and explain it," Jester said to the bear, looking rather shy at finding himself the centre of attention. "As a family grows, they pass on stories and things they've learned along the way." The more of them there are, the more you'll hear them say, *'they say'*."

Barely muttered something that sounded like, "harrumph," but continued to listen.

"We chipmunks teach our young that no one can tell, teach

or tattle if others aren't willing to listen, so it's best to only hear what's good, see what's right and say what's worth repeating." He finished this explanation in a rush and began busily licking his paws, then rubbed them nervously over his small, striped face, as if to hide away.

Smudge moved closer to the anxious chipmunk and looked down into his half-hidden eyes. Jester stopped his washing to look shyly back up at the bigger animal standing beside him.

"Thanks for sharing," Smudge said. "You're certainly one of the ones worth listening to."

The chipmunk bobbed his head several times in thanks. "I guess if other creatures joined us and wanted to learn too, we'd soon be telling them: 'well, you know what they say...Bastian buzzes beautifully!'" he chattered with a sudden laugh.

Bastian smiled and Smudge chuckled in appreciation, but Barely just shook his head as if trying to loosen something that had gotten stuck between his ears.

"Huh?" the bear grunted.

"He means we'd all be saying *'they say'* to each other," explained Bastian patiently.

"Oh. Now I get it. I told you I needed things explained over and over again. I guess I also need it explained in small bits like Jester does," sighed Barely.

"That's it in a nutshell!" exclaimed the chipmunk.

"What's that supposed to mean?" groaned the bear, lowering his head to the ground and covering it with two huge paws.

"Well, chipmunks are small and can't carry much more than a few nuts at a time, so we say that whatever fits inside a nutshell is about the right amount. I think it must be the same for you when you have to learn something," Jester replied.

"I guess so," Barely answered, uncovering his head.

"Jester, you know you aren't small at all, right? You're actually huge!" Bastian grinned. "At least to me. I'm glad you joined us. I think I've learned more today then in all my other days put together."

"I've learned about honey and nuts, so that makes it a good day for me too," Barely grunted. "But, hey, can we get on with lessons F and G before I fall asleep for the winter?"

"Should I go back to lesson A, perhaps?" Bastian wondered in a worried tone. "Maybe it would be better if I shared all twenty-six lessons from the beginning. Each have three except for F and G and–"

"No, that's way too many to learn!" interrupted Barely with a loud groan. "You sure are nuts about learning."

"Could be!" hummed Bastian, leaving the stump and zipping back and forth in excitement.

"I've always hated learning...well, almost always," Barely hastily corrected. "Maybe it was the way Mama bear growled on and on while I was trying to remember." The bear rose to full height once more, put one paw on his hip and began waggling the other huge paw in Smudge's face. His voice also rose to a high-pitched growl, as if trying to mimic his mother's tone. "Now don't forget this and don't forget that little cub," he warned.

The effect was so comical that they all burst out laughing.

"Hmph. That was Mama bear, always pushing me to learn more. The more she pushed the less I understood, and the more she growled the less I remembered."

"Well, you've remembered some of it, so her growling must have helped a bit," Jester suggested.

"A very little bit," grumbled Barely, dropping back to all fours.

"At least you had someone who loved you enough to want you to learn," Smudge pointed out.

"I suppose that is something," Barely reluctantly agreed.

"And it has helped keep you alive and safe all these years," Bastian pointed out.

"Well, if you're going to rub it in," Barely growled, pacing back and forth and looking none too happy.

"Let's get started on lesson F, shall we?" said Bastian, wisely changing the subject.

"About time," Barely muttered in a rather bearish manner, "and make it short and simple so I don't doze off, okay?"

"Alright," Bastion replied in a mild voice, although Smudge thought he saw a bit of a spark in her eye. "The first F lesson is an especially good one for you, Barely."

"Yeah? What is it?" he asked with a huge yawn, as if another lesson was the last thing he wanted to hear. He stared distractedly up into the branches of the fir tree, watching them wave about in the wind.

"It's *Focus*!" Bastian bellowed.

"Huh? What did you say?" Barely asked, dragging his eyes away from the tree back toward the black and yellow buzzing ball flying near his face.

Smudge and Jester began to giggle.

"*Focus*," she shouted again, hovering an inch from his snout. "It means to stay awake and pay attention when someone who cares about you is trying to teach you something important." Bastian stressed each word, saying it in a slow and somewhat mocking manner.

This caused the dog and chipmunk to chuckle even harder, holding their paws against their mouths as they tried without success to smother their laughter. As his friend's words and the accompanying laughter finally sank in, Barely's expression changed to one of hurt. He glanced away and the squeals and howls of laughter from the others faded. They were replaced by a guilty silence. After a moment Barely turned back, looking determined to be brave.

"And what's the second lesson?" he asked Bastian in a very low voice.

She flew to the ground and landed between the bear's heavily padded front paws.

"*Forgive*," she said softly. "It means to pardon someone who's hurt you. I'm sorry I said something that caused others to laugh at you, Barely. I shouldn't have been so unkind."

The bear looked hard at the bee, then at the dog and chipmunk, who were now sitting quietly together and looking very sorry.

"Well then, I forgive you," he said simply. "Now get on with telling us what great G lesson the hive teaches; I promise to focus and not fall asleep. If I do, you have permission to sting me. *Fall*, by the way, is one of the few bear essentials I do remember, since that's when we bears get ready for our long winter nap." He plunked his shaggy, brown frame down onto the ground and nudged the bee with his nose, murmuring to himself: "I probably need to start learning this stuff anyway before I get too much older."

Bastian hummed in delight at the return of Barely's good mood and flew several circles around his head.

"Thanks for forgiving me and for giving me permission to sting you." She smiled as the words twisted from her mouth. "Of course, I wouldn't do that now that I know you."

"Mama bear used to say we should go back and make amends whenever we could. That's another of our bear essentials. She said if you can't go back, just go forward and do it right the next time. Papa bear said the only time we needed to feel ashamed was when we understood we'd hurt someone and could have said sorry, but didn't."

"Some creatures hurt others on purpose just to be mean," Smudge remarked, thinking of Basher.

"True. But if they were truly sorry I think you'd still have to give them another chance," the bear grunted. "After all, we want others to give us that chance."

"Hmmm...Barely, I think you already know lesson G quite well," said Bastian.

"I do?" the bear asked, looking puzzled, but pleased.

"Sure. It's *Give*." Bastian hummed in merriment and Barely huffed along with her in bearish good humour.

"You had pretty smart parents," Jester said to the bear in admiration.

"I didn't think so when I was a cub," Barely responded. "Somehow, though, the older I get the smarter they seem."

"Maybe it's just that you're growing wiser," squeaked Jester with a wink.

"Maybe," the bear repeated rather doubtfully. "Anyway, I wish they were still around to growl at me." He wiped at one eye with a huge paw and added, "but at least I have friends who are patient enough to help an old bear like me remember a few bear essentials I'd forgotten. I think you'd all have made good bears."

"*Friends*. Now there's the most important F word every dog should know!" exclaimed Smudge.

"I think it should be part of our lessons too," echoed Bastian. "Hey, why don't you all come back to my hive for a quick visit?"

"Umm...er...ah...well..." the dog, chipmunk and bear all hummed and hawed while they shuffled and pawed at the ground.

"Alright, then give me a minute while I go spread the word to the other bees!" And off she flew to the flowers, buzzing loudly as she went.

"Wow! That bee is wise," said Smudge as he watched Bastian fly away.

"So are you," Jester told him.

"Me? I don't think so. Sometimes when my master gets mad at me he calls me a silly dog."

"That's not very good of him, but you shouldn't worry about the things others say when they're mad," Barely grunted. "Just because they call you a name, doesn't mean that's what you are. We know you're smart. Learning takes some of us longer than others, that's all. Your human probably just doesn't understand you yet."

"Well, as long as we work to understand each other in the end that's what really matters, right?" Jester asked.

"You bet," replied the bear. "I know I'm smarter today than I was yesterday, and it's because you've all been so patient with me."

"Maybe you need to be patient with yourself too," Smudge suggested. "When we look at ourselves and see something we don't like, we need to be patient and persevere at trying to change it."

"Or at least change the direction you're flying," Jester joked, flapping his small paws in the air as if he were a bird. "In my family we practice until we get good at things. We all need to practice patience when things are hard for us to understand."

Barely stretched out his back legs and gave another yawn. "Yeah...that's me. Hey, let's walk up the road a bit," he suggested.

Smudge gave a hesitant nod. He didn't usually leave home without a leash attached to his collar and his master holding onto the other end. He'd been given the order that he wasn't to go walking alone, but he was going to have his friends with him, so he decided it would be okay. With a sigh, he wondered how he could possibly explain such a thing as a leash to his companions, who came and went as they pleased.

"What's wrong?" the chipmunk enquired as they wandered through the dry grass by the side of the road.

"I think the thing I'm most afraid of is not being understood by others," Smudge admitted. He told them all about the leash, hoping they wouldn't laugh too much.

"I see what you mean," Barely replied. "I can't say I understand it, but as long as you and your master are okay with it, I guess we just have to respect it."

"I think Barely's right," Jester chattered in agreement. "We all have different ways. How does being on a leash feel to your stomach Smudge?"

"What kind of question is that?" Barely chortled. "Smudge doesn't wear the leash around his stomach!" He paused for a moment before looking at Smudge and asking, "Do you?"

"No," the dog confirmed. "And I don't quite know what you mean Jester."

"They say if you aren't sure that what you're doing is right or wrong to just ask your stomach," explained the chipmunk.

"*They* all sound a bit nutty to me!" the bear guffawed.

"I think I get what you mean now," Smudge said with a tilt of his head. "Whenever I'm doing something wrong I feel it deep inside, and it's the same when I'm doing something right. To me, walking on a leash with my master feels really right. He gives me everything I need to eat and drink after all, plus a warm, safe house to share. In return I'm obedient to him, which pleases him and makes me feel good too—not to mention it gets me more dog treats," he finished, licking his chops.

"I never thought of that," Barely said. "Maybe you're luckier than us, even though it means being on a leash sometimes."

"It does sound like a better life than running wild," Jester mused. "If I knew I had a master taking care of me I wouldn't worry so much. I wish we could be friends with your human too."

"My master told me a neat story about how, long ago, all the creatures on earth were friends with each other."

"Sounds great. I wonder if it could ever be that way again?" Barely considered with a hopeful look.

"If we keep being friends do you think your human might want to start being our friend too?" the chipmunk questioned. "He might even want to start helping us if we need it."

"I guess it could happen," Smudge said slowly. "He's a good human, and he really cares about me and about other humans, but I'm afraid it would take loads of patience and hard work on our part to help him understand that you might need his help too. It's probably best if we help each other for now. Maybe he'll learn by watching us."

"They say teaching by example is the best way to help others learn!" chirped the chipmunk.

The trio had stopped again, this time to wait for Bastian, and now sat soaking up the mild warmth offered by the autumn sun.

 # HONEY

"Hey, you aren't learning stuff without me, are you?" Bastian called out as she flew up the road to join them. She touched lightly on each creature's nose before landing gently on the ground. "Sorry I took so long to come back. I gathered some nectar and had to take it back to the hive. So, what was that I heard about hard work?"

"It's something you do way too much of already." Barely snorted. "Do you ever just stop to *smell* the flowers?"

"I think you're the one who's supposed to be doing that work," Smudge advised him. "I've heard that bears help spread flower pollen by sniffing them."

"It does stick to my nose quite often," confirmed Barely. "Tickles like crazy and makes me sneeze something awful. I didn't realize I was working when I did that. I thought work was something we don't like to do."

"Not if you're doing the work that's right for you," Bastian hummed, "and I see now that I have you to thank for some of the beautiful flowers that grow in the forest and meadows. It seems you've already done some work toward earning your share of the honey." She made an elaborate bee bow in front of him.

"Hmph. I haven't tasted any yet," he grumped, but in a good-natured sort of way. "Hey, wouldn't it be great if we could just have honey without all the hard work?" A dreamy look came over his face, as if he was actually picturing a golden river of free flowing sweetness.

"Hmmm...honey without working for it. It's a great dream, but in the end, someone has to do the work. If some bees did and others didn't, you'd end up with some pretty cranky worker bees," declared Bastian.

"Are there bees who think it isn't worth the work?" asked Jester.

"Yes, there are some who fly away as soon as they realize the effort they have to put in. Young bees are taught that honey is something the hive works for together, not something some bees work for to give to others while they buzz about having fun. They quickly learn that honey won't just keep flowing to them if they choose to play all day."

"Could it be the same way with everything?" Smudge wondered aloud. "I mean, if honey is the reward for a bee's efforts, maybe having friends who are willing to help us is our reward for the hard work of understanding others."

"Now that's something I'm willing to work for," chattered the chipmunk.

"And it sure would make life more peaceful," grunted the bear. "Of course, we'd have to hope that others were willing to put in the effort to understand us too."

"Give them a taste of honey so they know what they're working for...or choosing to give up," suggested Bastian.

"A taste of friendship," Smudge nodded slowly. "What a good idea. After that it's up to them to decide whether we're worth the effort or not."

"And if they don't, what should we do?" Jester queried.

"Feel sorry for them, I guess," Smudge replied, "and be willing to take them back if they ever want to try again, especially if they moved away because we were hard to understand."

"You're right, Smudge," Bastian said, giving him a sweet smile, "since some of us are much harder to understand than others."

"That would be me," grunted the bear. "My greatest fear is that you'll all run away from me if I forget myself and really growl at you."

"Knowing your fear helps us understand you better," stated the chipmunk in a serious voice, pulling at his small ears.

"If everyone just told each other that to start with we could save ourselves a mound of trouble," grumbled the bear.

"If it were easy to do we probably would," Smudge pointed out; "but, as long as we do in the end, that's what matters."

"Exactly! Which means hard work!" Bastian buzzed, determined to have the last word.

 L

"Grr! Can't you ever stop talking about work?" demanded Barely with a sharp growl. He stopped halfway through to clamp a huge paw over his mouth. "Sorry for growling," he apologized to her in a far gentler tone. "It's just that, if all you ever do is work, you might end up doing, but never being."

"Huh?" Bastian buzzed in confusion. It was quite unusual to see her not understand something, and she began flying in wild circles, obviously feeling some upset about this.

Smudge felt sorry for her, since he'd often felt the same way.

"I think Barely means that it's important to stop doing things sometimes and live without running in circles," explained Jester to the agitated bee.

"I don't run in circles!" Bastian exclaimed, doing a dizzying series of spins. "I don't run at all!"

"Ah, but you fly in circles!" the bear quickly pointed out.

"I like running in circles," Smudge muttered under his breath to a nearby clump of grass.

Barely ignored his comment and looked up to where the bee had now stopped, mid-flight, and hovered like a tiny, quivering speck against the sky. It was easy to see that she was struggling to remain still.

"Bastian, you almost never seem to stop moving around, busy doing this and that. Why is it that bees can't seem to stop and just be?" He gave a lopsided grin to show his words were kindly meant and only said out of concern for her.

"I want to do more than simply be," Bastian stated firmly, and turned to fly farther up the road. The others followed her lead, sauntering along at an easier pace.

"Coming from you, that sounds pretty funny," the bear shouted out after her.

Bastian looked back with a smile, her good humour returning. It was clear she liked the bear enough to listen to what he had to say, and so hadn't taken any real offence at his words.

"It's part of lesson L," she called out to them, then landed on a branch and waited until they'd caught up before adding: *"Look in, Look up, Look out. If you only do one or two of those, you miss out on so much."*

"Hurrah. Another lesson," chuckled the bear.

"If you don't look up you won't ever see the sun," Jester pointed out.

"And if you don't look in you'll never really understand yourself," said the bee.

"I suppose if you don't look out you won't understand anybody else either," Barely concluded.

"Or be able to help them," Smudge added. "Bastian, shouldn't looking in also mean looking at how we can make ourselves better?"

"Of course! It doesn't matter if we can't change what we are, so long as we can change the direction we fly."

"If we don't understand ourselves we might be moving in the wrong direction without even knowing it," said the bear as he scratched at his furry head.

"Hmmm, that wouldn't be good, since it could lead to hurting others," Bastian replied.

"Well, knowing you're a bear doesn't mean you're going to be able to just stop growling, even if you want to," Barely replied. "I've been trying for awhile now, but it still keeps slipping out."

"Nobody should get mad if they know you're really trying," Jester consoled him.

"Bastian and I were talking about that before you joined us," Smudge said.

The bee nodded her tiny head. "Smudge wanted to know the point of trying to change into something else if you know you're a dog and will always be a dog."

Barely gave a loud snort. "Hmph! That sounds like giving up to me. Other bears might tell you there's no point in trying to change and become less bear-like. They'd say it's a waste of time and can't be done. And look at what else they've told me couldn't be done. They've said bears and bees can't be friends, yet I've made a bee-friend today who's willing to share her honey with me in exchange for just a little bit of work—"

At these words, Bastian began buzzing loudly and zoomed at the bear's head.

Barely ducked and hastily backed up, calling out: "Ahem... I meant plenty of good, *hard* work, of course!"

Bastian swerved away and Barely lifted his head back up, his face bearing a wide grin. "As I was saying," he continued, "no other bear is going to believe a bee and bear could be such good friends without seeing it for themselves. That means I'd better keep trying to change in other ways too, to show them anything is possible."

"I think you're quite wise, Barely," Jester chattered, laying a hesitant paw on the huge bear. "My family is the reason why it's important for me to keep trying, no matter how hard it is or how often I fail. Otherwise, what example would they have to follow?"

"Those are both great reasons," Smudge said to the chipmunk and bear. "For me it's more about not disappointing my master. He expects so much from me, yet gives so much more in return that it just makes me want to keep trying until I learn what's important to him and get it right. What about you Bastian? Why do you try so hard?"

The bee buzzed about in an intricate series of circles before coming back to hover mode.

"Because the sun's shining in the sky. When the clouds get in the way and the rain and snow comes or on dark winter nights, I remind myself that the sun will come back again. Just because we try and fail, doesn't mean we'll keep failing if we keep trying. You can't help but succeed if you remember the sun."

"Sounds good to me," Smudge barked.

Bastian began to fly in happy loops again, as if this kind of sharing made her want to fly higher. "Lesson L is the best! *Look in, Look up, and Look out!*" she buzzed loudly as she completed each one.

"*Look in* to see how you can change for the better!"

shouted Smudge in response.

"*Look up* because the sun's shining down on you whether you see it or not!" chimed the chipmunk.

"*Look out* to see how you can help others!" boomed the bear.

"Exactly!" Bastian buzzed more loudly than they'd yet heard.

"And for that we have to listen," Barely continued in a quieter voice. "*Listen* and *Learn*. Those are two more bear essentials I remember from when I was a cub. Papa bear taught me to listen to what the forest was saying, learn from it and never take it for granted."

"We teach those same things to our young," Jester piped up. "And, of course, everyone knows what they say about listening and learning." He paused a moment, but no one volunteered a guess. "Why they say we aren't likely to learn anything new if the only one we'll listen to is ourselves!" he supplied the answer for them. Springing onto a nearby log and standing his tallest (which wasn't very tall) he added: "We chipmunks don't have such things as lessons from the hive, a dog's important words or bear essentials, but if we did, when it comes to L, we'd have to choose *Love*."

"How come?" Smudge asked him.

"Because they say that, no matter what, where or when, families are supposed to love each other. Sometimes it feels like love disappears, but it's just like the sun behind the clouds; it's still there, even when you can't see it."

"Jester, you're so good at making hard things easier to understand," Smudge complimented. At that moment, his stomach interrupted their conversation with a loud rumble, causing the dog to recall his missed noonday meal. He decided he could ignore the feeling of hunger for a while longer.

"The important L words I learned as a puppy were *Lunch* and *Look out,*" he continued. "Lunch was easy to learn, but look out sure didn't mean the same thing as it does in Bastian's lesson."

"What else could it mean?" enquired the curious bee.

"It's what my master says when he wants me to run away from something that scares him. I think that's how I learned to be so afraid."

"You probably need to help him learn courage by not running away yourself," Bastian suggested.

"Yup, I've been thinking that too," Smudge replied.

"I think you're right," Jester agreed with them. "Hopefully I've set a good example for my family by coming here today. It took all my courage, because I thought the food might be a trap."

"What if it had been?" the bear asked. "You wouldn't have known until it was too late!"

Smudge hung his head in shame. "I might have done that before I realized Jester was taking our seeds and carrots without understanding how they got there," he admitted.

"Well, if I'd known how hard you'd worked to grow them I

sure wouldn't have taken them," the chipmunk said, looking just as sorry. "If I'd known how kind you were, I would have been brave enough to come forward much sooner."

"There! That proves courage is about taking a chance!" exclaimed Bastian, beating her wings as hard as she could. An unexpected gust of wind was blowing by, and it suddenly seemed to be taking all her efforts to remain close to the group.

 # TO RUN OR NOT TO RUN

As if spurred on by the challenge of staying in one place against the force of the strong breeze, Bastian began to move even faster. By the time the gust had passed she'd launched into a frenzied figure eight pattern that was dizzying to watch.

The others looked on in awe as she whipped in circles above their heads. Smudge wasn't aware of it, but his head was tilted to one side again, as if trying to figure out everything he could about the tiny bee's excitable nature. He noticed Barely shaking his head the way he usually did when he didn't quite get something, and Jester was pulling fretfully at his ears, perhaps so he could hear better anything that Bastian might say.

After awhile Bastian slowed her pace, until finally she was moving in the kind of lazy loops bees are sometimes known to make on hot, summer afternoons.

Smudge decided he preferred this slower flying pattern, since it was easier for his eyes to follow. He could hear Bastian humming softly to herself.

"Sometimes it hurts when someone gets too close to us," Barely boomed, ducking again as the bee flew a bit too close to his eyes.

Bastian startled, as if she'd forgotten about her friends for a moment. She did a back flip and zipped off in the other direction.

Quickly turning back, she grinned and called out, "Too true. It's much easier to love someone when they're far away!"

"Really? Then perhaps we should move far enough away from others until we can see the good in them," Jester suggested.

"Smart thinking," grunted the bear, "but don't run or you might get chased."

"My master often says if you don't want to slip, don't run on ice," Smudge murmured, staring off into the distance. He gave his head a shake, as if to wake himself up, and added, "I guess it's probably safest not to run at all, either toward or away from someone."

"Then how come you ran from Basher when you first met?" Bastian challenged him.

"That was different," Smudge defended himself. "Basher wanted to take a bite out of me." He quickly told the chipmunk and bear about the big dog next door. "...And I don't think it's about guarding what's his. It's about being a bully and letting the other neighbourhood dogs know it," he finished.

"I bet he *is* guarding something," Jester argued. "I bet he's guarding his reputation as top dog because he's afraid one of you might find out he isn't really so tough and might start bullying him, instead of the other way around."

"I never thought of that," admitted Smudge. "But then there's no point in my trying to make friends again if he won't let me get close enough to find out anything good about him."

"You did the right thing in the first place by trying to introduce yourself to him and it's still your choice whether to keep trying to make friends or give up," Jester responded.

"Basher may be a big dog while you're just a little one, but you've plenty of bark," the bear pointed out. "Besides, what's the worst he could possibly do to you when you have friends like us about?"

"Bite me. Hard." Smudge gave a shiver as he spoke.

"At least then you'd have it over with," Barely replied. "It might hurt for a bit before it healed, but I'll bet worrying about it hurts you even more."

Smudge looked up at the bear in wonder. He recalled Bastian having said something similar that morning and it was true that the thought of getting bitten by Basher had scared the little dog for a long time. This idea that he should just stand up to the dog next door and get it over with filled Smudge with a strange, new feeling.

"It's called courage, Smudge," Bastian said, flying close once more. "Once you accept the worst than can happen and face it, you'll find the fear has far less power over you."

Smudge slowly nodded. It was odd, but the more he thought about standing up to Basher, the braver he felt.

"What I'd like to know is, why do some creatures only seem to feel good when they can make others feel bad?" Bastian questioned.

"I wish I knew," Smudge shrugged.

"The ones to be really careful of are the hunters," Jester whispered nervously, as if suddenly remembering how defence-less he was. He cast an anxious look about and then glanced warily toward both dog and bear. "When they see you, they see supper. If you don't fight back you're lost," he added.

The bear paid no attention to either the look or comment, making Smudge wonder if being ignored wasn't sometimes a good thing. He threw Jester an encouraging smile and wagged his tail to show he was the same friendly dog who was willing to share his food.

"You can't always tell which they are until they're quite close," he said to the chipmunk, "but the proof is in what they do."

"Or don't do," chimed the tiny bee.

"So what should we do if we don't figure it out until it's too late?" Jester shivered.

"Bark really loud and run away," Smudge told him.

"Or buzz at the top of your voice, but only sting if you absolutely have to," suggested Bastian.

"Stand as tall as you can, growl for all your worth, and swat hard," Barely rumbled. He caught Bastian's eye and hastily added: "But only if you absolutely have to."

The three friends looked at each other then down at the small chipmunk. It seemed they were having the same sudden moment of understanding about what it must be like to be as defenceless as a chipmunk. Bastian broke the silence that followed.

"Turn to face what you're afraid of, especially if it's close to you," she cautioned the chipmunk, "and if it moves around you, turn to face it again. That's your best chance."

"Take your time about getting close to other creatures," the bear added his advice to that of the bee.

"They do say to take hard things one step at a time," said Jester with a quite air, starting to sound more confident.

"My master says to look hard at others, past smiles and handshakes, if you want to be sure of them," Smudge put in.

"What's a handshake?" questioned the chipmunk.

"It's like shaking paws or touching noses," the dog explained.

"Oh." Jester lifted a small paw up to his mouth to lick it, stopping half way up to note: "Well, you know what they say: eyes are windows to what's inside."

"And also mirrors to show us how we look to others,"

Smudge added.

"Mama and Papa bear used to say that very thing!" Barely exclaimed. "Now that's a point they could agree on—that, and honey."

Bastian hummed with pleasure at the compliment.

"I guess we all need to be careful we meet someone new," Smudge said decidedly, "but still brave enough to move forward."

"That's right," Bastian said in agreement. "Courage isn't just about facing your fear. It's also about being able to take action if necessary."

"That's important," Jester confirmed, bobbing his small head up and down in a rapid motion. He smoothed back the fur on his head then asked. "So, is there any fear we should hold onto?"

"Definitely," rumbled the bear, swaying his huge, brown body from side to side. "The fear of hurting others."

Bastian flew over to the bear and landed on his ear, humming softly as she did so. Smudge nodded his head and Jester moved two steps closer to the huge beast.

"They say it's better to be respected than liked," he chattered.

"Great. All Smudge has to do is find a way to make Basher respect him," the bear pronounced.

Smudge scowled when he heard this, but Bastian backed the bear's comment, saying, "He's right Smudge. You just need to find a way to make Basher respect you."

"And hey, there's always the chance he won't bite you," grunted the brown bear, shaking his huge rump as if some small bug was biting him. "After all, even I growled at you when we first met, but I didn't hurt you. Maybe he's all bark and no bite."

"He might be," Smudge sighed, watching as the bear moved restlessly from side to side.

"But just to be on the safe side, make sure you're a faster runner than he is," Barely cautioned, leaning back and scratching at his hindquarters with sharp claws.

"Good point," Smudge replied, "and it reminds me of a story I once heard about a race between a tortoise and—"

"A what?" the bear broke in, scratching madly as his flanks.

"A tortoise. It's kind of like a turtle only huge—" Smudge started to explain, but the bear cut in a second time.

"As huge as me?" he demanded, sitting down and rubbing his back end against the ground in an effort to erase the sudden itch.

"No, more about my size and—"

"But you aren't huge," the bear interrupted yet again.

"Oh, just let him tell the story," Jester scolded.

"I had to make sure I understood," the brown bear growled, continuing to paw at whatever itched him.

"That's okay," Smudge nodded. "Anyway, this sort of over-sized turtle and this hare..." he paused to glance at the bear before hurrying on, "which is sort of like a rabbit, except it has longer ears and is a bit bigger...met one day and they—"

"How big?" Barely cut him off, then gave a loud chuckle. "Just kidding. Go on with your story. A huge turtle as big as you and a sort of large rabbit...what comes next?"

Smudge gave a good-natured sigh and looked for a comfortable spot to sit. He chose a patch of ground beneath a fair-sized alder, still thick with leaves, though many had already fallen to the ground. Barely followed him and immediately began rubbing his back against the tree's bark, snorting loudly as he finally found some relief. Bastian had remained with the bear up until that point, but when he began using the tree as a scratching post she left this perch to fly over to Jester. The chipmunk had just scurried up to join the group when Bastian landed unexpectedly on his nose. Startled, he jumped back, and Bastian lost her balance and fell. She caught herself before hitting the ground, though, and flew up to hover in front of the chipmunk. Jester nodded his permission for her to land again and she immediately settled on the tip of his nose, keeping her stinger high so that she didn't hurt him.

"You shouldn't have startled me like that" he scolded her, keeping his nose quite steady so she wouldn't fall again.

"Sorry," apologized the tiny bee. "I wanted to stay close by so I didn't miss any of the story."

"Me too," he told her. "Smudge do go on. What happened when they met?"

"Okay," the dog began again, "the rabbit challenged the turtle to a race to see who'd win and—"

"What? Why, that's just silly!" shouted the bear, stopping his scratching for a brief moment. "A turtle could never beat a rabbit!"

"It's never, never!" three voices corrected him.

"And there's an exception to every rule," he reminded them in turn.

"Okay, but the turtle really did beat the rabbit, Barely. Want to know how?" Smudge grinned.

The huge bear nodded, saying not a word.

"Well, the rabbit moved really fast and the turtle pretty slow, but the turtle won in the end because the rabbit did some silly things."

"Like what?" Barely demanded.

"He got so far ahead of the turtle he thought it safe to stop and play for awhile."

"That isn't silly at all. It seems reasonable that, since the rabbit was so far ahead, he should have had some time to play," murmured the chipmunk, who loved taking time to play with his young family.

"Yes, but then he took a long nap," Smudge added.

"Nothing wrong with that," Barely said with a huge yawn and a stretch. "So, how did this huge turtle win?"

"He just kept plodding on, not stopping to play or rest."

"Why, how sensible! It's obvious the turtle's perseverance won the race in the end," droned the worker bee.

"I think you're all right," Smudge said thoughtfully. "Playing, resting and plodding on to make sure we get the job done are all important, but none is more important than the other. The story is meant to teach us about how to keep going, even when winning seems unlikely and the race is really hard. But what we win or lose may be more important than just winning by itself."

"It doesn't seem like the turtle won much of anything, except being able to boast a bit," Barely pointed out.

"And the rabbit only lost a bit of his pride, which was probably a good thing," Bastian added.

"But think about what they could have won!" Smudge barked in excitement. "If they'd helped each other to the finish line, they both could have got there sooner."

"How could they possibly have helped each other?" questioned the bear.

"Perhaps the huge turtle could have offered to let the rabbit take a nap on his shell so he didn't fall behind while he slept," suggested Jester.

"Or maybe the big rabbit could have picked the turtle up and run with him to the finish line," said Bastian.

"If they'd worked together, they both could have ended up with more time to play and rest without losing the race," the bear grunted, looking surprised at having figured it out.

"Exactly!" exclaimed Smudge. "They both would have won! In the end, I think it matters more that we help each other get to the finish line than who crosses first."

"Does that mean we should run toward something if it's good and run away if it's bad?" asked Jester.

"Hmmm...if you put it that way, my answer would be yes," replied Smudge.

"Just keep in mind that we can't always tell what's good or bad if we haven't taken the time to really understand it," Bastian reminded them.

Jester looked thoughtfully at the bee perched on the end of his nose, as if trying to figure out how her words could help him. He raised a small paw and absently pulled at one ear, causing the bee to lose her balance again and take flight. She moved to a large twig, which had broken off the tree during Barely's scratching marathon, and resettled herself.

"If we really want to help each other to the finish line we need to be brave enough to stay and help those who need us..." Smudge began, then stopped as a sudden thought occurred to him. Maybe Basher really needed help and didn't know how to ask for it.

"Don't run away, Smudge," Bastian said softly, as if reading his mind.

"What if I did stay to try and help, but only managed to make things worse?" he asked her.

"I'd think no less of you," Bastian replied. "It's always harder to stay than it is to run. For that you should be proud."

Smudge walked over to where Bastian sat and gently nudged her with his nose as his way of saying thank you.

"Wait a minute! I thought it was never always?" boomed Barely, hardly able to hide a huge grin behind his paw.

The others laughed.

"And now we know what the turtle and rabbit would have won if they'd worked together," the chipmunk piped up.

"We do?" Barely asked, scratching his head and looking puzzled.

"Sure," Jester replied. "Great friends."

"And their friendship might have helped them to understand something better than they did to start with," Smudge added.

Barely sighed, as if this guessing game was getting to be too much for him. "Like what?" he asked wearily.

"Each other!" Smudge exclaimed. "Now that is what my master would call a fairy-tale."

"A what?" both Jester and Bastian enquired.

"No!" the bear groaned, cowering down and covering his head with his paws. "Please don't tell us what that means."

"A fairy-tale is a made up story about things that couldn't possibly be true," Smudge explained anyway.

Barely groaned louder, tossing his head from side to side, as if he'd been stung by a bee. No one spoke for a bit except the wind, which had begun to blow a little harder against the four companions gathered together beneath the alder tree. Several leaves were pulled unwillingly from its branches and spun this way and that before finally falling to the ground.

Barely raised his head, then his body, until he once more towered above them. Taking a deep breath, as if he was about to plunge into a pool of icy water, he cautiously asked, "Like what? What things that couldn't possibly be true?"

"Well, humans flying without wings, for instance, or creatures that can make themselves completely invisible or..." Smudge paused briefly to give them a wink of his eye, "...like animals being able to talk to each other."

Bastian immediately began to buzz and Jester to giggle, then laugh out load as they realized what he was saying. It took Barely a few moments longer to get it, but when he did he too began to grin, then chuckle, then at last fell back to the ground, overcome with laughter.

"Your human really thinks we can't talk?" giggled Jester.

"Yup. He says things like: 'Smudge, sometimes I really think you're trying to tell me something,' or, 'too bad dogs can't talk'." Smudge howled.

"Oh, you're making my sides split," gasped Barely, holding his stomach as he rocked back and forth.

"Too funny!" Bastian echoed, taking to the air and spinning in a series of wild, upside down loops.

Soon they all had tears running down their faces as they howled, rumbled, squealed and buzzed with laughter. It was some time before they managed to contain their merriment.

"Wow, laughing sure makes me hungry," Barely wheezed, wiping at his eyes with the back of one paw. His stomach gave a loud growl for all to hear. "And that confirms it," he chortled.

"I have an idea. Wait here," Bastian commanded and off she flew.

Her friends watched her disappear then sat down to await her return in the now much cooler afternoon air.

"Smudge curled up into a ball amongst the fallen leaves as he too began to think about food. He'd missed his lunch, but wasn't feeling quite ready to return to the house just yet. He began licking his paws in an effort to forget the pangs of hunger rumbling in the pit of his stomach and watched as Jester began searching under the fallen leaves.

"He's probably feeling the same way and trying to find a seed to munch," thought Smudge. But he was wrong.

The chipmunk came to a spot that seemed of particular interest to him and began to dig. Moments later he uncovered half of what might once have been an apple. Brushing the dirt off, he dragged the old piece of fruit over to Barely and placed it between his huge paws before scampering back to Smudge to ask, "Are you hungry too?"

Smudge patted his small friend on the head and assured him he was not. It was taking the dog a fair amount of effort to ignore the rumblings in his stomach, since he was used to having food handy whenever he might want some, but he didn't want the chipmunk to use up any more of his family's food supply.

"Thanks! That was really sweet," boomed the bear, licking the last of the juice from his paws.

"It was the last one hanging on a tree in Smudge's yard," Jester said, then looked horrified, as if realizing to whom the tree must belong.

"It's okay," Smudge assured him. "My master's finished his fruit picking for the year, so you can have whatever's left on our trees. He can't reach the really high ones anyway."

"I can," squeaked the chipmunk. "This one was hanging way out on a slender bit of branch, but it was worth the effort."

"Really? And you went out and picked it? You could have fallen!" the bear gasped. He loved climbing trees, but was very afraid of going out on a branch and falling.

"I know, but if we want the fruit we have to be willing to go out onto a limb to get it," advised the brave little chipmunk.

Their conversation was interrupted by the sound of a bevy of buzzing and Bastian reappeared, followed by several bees from her hive. Each carried a single honeycomb filled to the brim with liquid honey. She introduced them to her new friends, then instructed Barely to stand quite still with mouth opened wide. He did so without question. The bees lined up and began a fly-by, dropping their tiny gifts onto the brown bear's huge, pink tongue. As each honeycomb landed he swallowed, licked his lips and called out, "Oh, how delicious! Perfect! Excellent! Thank you friends! Thank you!"

The bees danced in delight on hearing such praise, seeming very pleased. When they were done, they grouped back together for a final whirl above his head, and then buzzed off, leaving Bastian alone with her companions once more.

"I've talked to the queen bee about you and she asked if you could come by the hive early tomorrow to start your guarding," Bastian said, hovering before the bear. "She thought it a splendid way to save us from having to sting any more honey thieves."

"I'll be there!" Barely replied with his usual lopsided grin. "I must say, this 'friends' thing is working out great!"

"Especially if they're kind enough to share," Jester said, looking gratefully toward Smudge. "Thanks again for the carrots and crust of bread."

Smudge nodded back, saying, "Those are some of my favourites, along with cheese, marmalade and oranges." His tail wagged in fond memory of the mouth-watering foods.

"Oranges? However do you eat a colour?" Jester asked curiously, sitting back down to listen.

"What's a colour?" the dog replied in confusion.

"Wait a minute. Are you saying you don't know about colour?" Bastian called out.

"I'm saying I don't understand what you're asking me about," Smudge said hesitantly. "I was talking about food."

Barely snuffed loudly, then drummed his claws against his mouth a few times, as if carefully considering the situation. "Smudge," he finally asked, "when you eat an orange, what do you see?"

The dog tilted his head to one side. "A round ball," he replied.

"Round like an apple?" Barely questioned.

"Yes, mostly, but darker than some and lighter than others. It smells way different, though, and tastes even better; it's as sweet as honey."

"That's probably because of the bees," Bastian explained. "They love the nectar from orange tree blossoms. My cousins down south boast that, if it weren't for them, there wouldn't be any oranges at all."

"What are you all talking about?" Jester broke in, wringing his paws together and looking very confused. "Orange is a colour, not a food!"

"It's food to me," Smudge explained, then suddenly jumped to his feet as a new thought occurred to him. "Hey, why don't I just bring a piece of orange for you to try the next time I get one?" he offered, realizing how hard Jester was struggling to get what they meant. It seemed they were speaking of a food he'd never seen or tasted, after all. Smudge's confusion over this thing they called 'colour' had given him a taste of the difficulty the chipmunk must be having.

Jester bobbed his head thankfully in response to the kind offer. "That would sure help," he said, looking quite relieved, then he too jumped to his feet. "Hey, if there's a food called orange, is there one called red? That's my favourite colour, along with green, orange and yellow."

"Not that I've ever heard—" Smudge began to say, but was cut off by Bastian, whose turn it was to look confused.

"What colour is red?" she asked.

"Oh no! Here we go again," groaned the bear, but this time he waddled over to where the bee hung suspended in the air, and began to explain as good-naturedly as his gruff character would allow. "Okay, red is...red, which is darker than orange and...lighter than brown."

He spoke slowly and Bastian waited patiently for him to continue. It took Barely a moment to figure out she needed more information and he gave his head a shake, as if to clear away cobwebs. "Apples can be red," he began again. "That's probably why some of them look darker to Smudge. The lighter ones are probably the yellows and greens."

Smudge's ears perked up in sudden understanding, but Bastian continued to stare blankly at the bear with a look that plainly said she still didn't get it.

"The sky can look red and some leaves turn red in the fall," Barely explained further.

Bastian sadly shook her head.

"Bastian, surely you've seen red flowers before?" Jester asked.

"How would I know if I don't know what they look like?" she asked in turn.

Barely gave a rough sigh, as if teaching others was something he found hugely difficult, but his determination to help was obvious, and he tried once more. "Bastian, what's your favourite color?" he enquired, taking a different approach to the matter.

"Oh, that's easy. White, of course!" the buzzy bee exclaimed. "Isn't it everyone's?"

"Actually, they say white isn't a colour, but a mix of all colours," the chipmunk spouted.

"They do?" Barely asked in surprise.

Jester bobbed his head up and down.

"Now, I'm not saying they aren't right Jester, but I can tell you that, seen through my eyes, white is only one colour and the most beautiful of all," Bastian told them. "It glows with a most wonderful light, especially when the sun shines."

Smudge approached the bee as she hovered happily in the air and she promptly folded back her wings to land on his nose.

"I sure wish I could see white through your eyes, Bastian. It sounds great," he murmured, looking a bit wistful that he'd never be able to see what she saw.

"Having different eyes means we see things differently; it gives us something to share," she gently reminded him. "I wish I could see things through your eyes too."

The little dog smiled at his bee friend, realizing the wisdom of her words. "I think I've figured out one way in which we're all exactly the same," he told her.

"Really? What's that?" Bastian asked, intrigued.

"We're all the same in that we're completely different! Whether it's how we see, smell, hear, taste, or feel, it seems none of us are exactly alike," he replied.

"Or meant to be," added Jester.

"What would we talk about if we were all exactly the same?" Barely snorted.

"Not much," Bastian answered. "We'd have nothing to share; nothing to learn. It would be pretty lonely."

"I'm glad we're all different," Smudge said, rising to his feet. He gave his nose a playful toss, launching Bastian back into the air.

She laughed, and began to dart about once more, her transparent wings moving so fast they were almost invisible. "Well, whatever you are, be the best you can be," she sang out.

"Is that what they say in your hive?" Jester questioned.

"No. They say be the best bee you can be," she called down from ten feet above his head.

"Oh great...that's probably lesson B," moaned the bear.

"You're partly right. Lesson B is very close to that," Bastian droned in pleased surprise.

"Do tell!" the dog and chipmunk cried out together.

Bastian dropped back down to their level, which made Barely back away. He didn't seem at all eager to hear what she had to say, and with a loud grunt leaned against the alder tree, ignoring them as he again began scratching his back against the rough bark.

Bastian didn't look at all upset by his actions, having become used to his bearish ways. In fact, she began doing another waggle dance to show how pleased and willing she was to share yet another lesson.

"*Beloved*," she sang out once she'd finished her dance. "That's the first of three from lesson B."

"Oh, that's a great one! It means to be loved by family," squeaked Jester. "And friends like you," he added shyly. "You've all been so kind and have helped me understand so many new things."

Barely made a muffled noise and turned away, but not before Smudge saw him wipe away an unexpectedly huge tear. "Never thought I'd care whether a chipmunk felt loved by me or not," he growled hoarsely. "Now everyone be quiet so Bastian can talk. Get on with that next lesson, bee....I sure hope there aren't more than three!"

"Why, Barely, you're starting to rhyme your words. For a moment you sounded just like Bastian, only bigger," Smudge teased him.

The bear gave a soft growl to show he wasn't pleased with being compared to a tiny bee, but Smudge wasn't afraid. He went over and nudged his little shoulder against one of the bear's huge back legs. Barely responded by playfully swatting him away while continuing to rub his bear back against the tree bark in an effort to finish his scratch."

"Go on little dog," he grunted with a grin, "or that dratted bee will never tell us the rest of the B lessons."

"*Believe*," Bastian buzzed loudly, flying a zigzag pattern between the three animals.

"Believe what?" questioned Smudge.

"It's the second of the bee's B lessons," she explained.

"I don't believe it," Barely joked, continuing his scratch-athon.

"So what should we believe in?" Jester asked her in a small, serious voice.

"Believe in love!" she hummed. "Believe in yourself! Believe in others! Believe in giving! Believe in miracles! Believe the sun still shines in the sky when we can't see it! Just believe!"

"Well, that certainly covers everything," Barely said with a grunt. However, he did stop his scratching so he could pay more attention.

"I believe in *Breakfast*," chuckled Smudge. "That's the most important B word for dogs, and my master says it's the most important meal of the day."

"Every meal is important to a bear," Barely huffed, "so I guess you could say I believe in food."

"It's a start," beamed Bastian.

"They say starting small is better than never starting at all," quoted Jester, his small, bushy tail waving slightly in the wind. "As for me, if two days ago someone had said Smudge and I would end up being friends I'd never have believed them."

"Me neither," Smudge agreed, sitting down beside the chipmunk. "Bastian, you seem to believe in way more than we do. How can you be so sure of everything?"

Three pairs of eyes locked onto the bee, waiting for her reply. She flew to a rather sorry looking flower of white, now past its prime, its once pretty face hanging limp and bowed, and drooping so low it brushed the ground.

"Because of the flowers," she explained simply. "They choose to open, believing the light of the sun will be there to greet them and life-giving water will fall from the sky."

"I bet they hope for gentle rain," murmured Smudge, thinking of how much he disliked getting wet.

"Very likely, but even harsh rain gives them what they need," Bastian replied.

"Frost and snow mean their end," Jester noted. "I doubt they'd be so willing to open up if they realized how much they could get hurt."

"If fear of what might hurt them kept them from opening they'd never blossom," Bastian pointed out.

As Barely listened to this exchange, a look of horror came over his face. "Never blossom?" he shouted. "Why, that would be terrible! The bees wouldn't have any nectar and there'd be no honey for bee or bear!"

Bastian hurriedly flew over to the agitated bear and landed on his right ear, humming softly in an attempt to soothe him. "But they do blossom," her sweet voice reminded him. "They take a chance and open up. If you begin each day that way you'll soon find yourself believing too."

"Oh...Hey, I get it!" Barely rumbled in a surprised tone.

Jester just looked thoughtful, but didn't speak. Smudge seemed to be considering what the bee had said and several moments passed by before he spoke.

"I think I know what you mean Bastian," he finally declared. "From now on I'll remember water is a good thing, no matter how afraid of baths I might be...Hey, speaking of water, look at those clouds. I bet there's rain in them."

Bastian gave a buzz and moved into the shelter of Barely's ear.

They had been so enjoying their time together none had noticed the change of weather. Now they could see that the large cloud, which had been sitting placidly on the horizon as the day began, had slowly crept forward, so that now it half covered the face of the sun. A few solitary raindrops fell, and Smudge scrambled to his feet.

"I should hurry home," he said with a worried woof.

The others, who were used to being out in all kinds of weather, looked up at the sky, then at the dog, as if they didn't quite understand his concern, but, being his friends, were willing to try.

"And I should head off to find more food," Barely stated, raising his shaggy form. "Come on Smudge, I'll walk you home."

The chipmunk nodded, following the others as they left the shelter of the alder tree and moved back toward the road.

 # SHADOWS

As the four companions moved out of the cloud's shadow and back into the remaining sunlight, Smudge sighed. "At least when it's cloudy there aren't any shadows," he said.

"Shadows aren't anything to worry about," Barely stated in bafflement.

"I've been afraid of them my whole life," Smudge admitted in a lowered voice, frightened the grey spectres might overhear him. "When I saw your shadow against the house a few nights ago it looked twice your size. I think I was more scared of it than of you, and I was plenty scared of you."

Bastian left her perch inside Barely's ear and came to fly alongside Smudge.

"Whether big or small, they're only a reflection of something else," she explained. "Look at the shadow you're making now."

Smudge looked over his shoulder and saw a little dog lying on the rock next to him. Whichever way he moved, the shadow dog moved too.

"That's not really you, just a copy of what you look like when you block the sun, the same as that cloud's trying to do," chattered Jester, pointing upward.

"Try moving so that you see your shadow from a different angle," Bastian suggested.

Smudge did as instructed and his shadow grew slightly larger. "Hey, it changed!" he exclaimed.

"Of course; and if we were able to look directly at the sun, all the shadows would disappear completely," Bastian explained.

"Oh, never do that!" Smudge warned her. "My master says it will hurt your eyes."

"I've heard that too," Barely grunted. "I wonder if shadows are there to distract us so we don't get hurt by looking at something too bright to see?"

"I suppose that's possible," Jester answered him. "They say shadows are liars. Maybe that's because they lie on the ground, or perhaps it's because they aren't real by themselves and don't reflect things as they truly are. Either way, without light, they couldn't exist."

"Smudge, you wouldn't want the light to go away just to get rid of the shadows, would you?" Bastian coaxed.

Smudge reluctantly shook his head.

"Anyway, shadows can't hurt you," Barely rumbled. "When the sun gets too hot in the summer I go looking for the shadows beneath trees so I can cool down."

"That's smart," agreed Smudge, who didn't like being out in the summer sun past high noon, when it got too hot to sleep comfortably. "I guess daytime shadows are okay. It's more the night-time shadows that scare me."

"Really?" Jester asked in surprise. "Night shadows don't frighten me at all. When I see them it means there's a light shining somewhere to help me find my way home."

"Shadows are my good friends," Barely spoke up. "It gets lonely at night in the forest when you don't have family around. Sometimes I feel like the shadows are dancing with me or playing tricks to make me laugh. I like it when they keep me company because then I don't feel so alone."

"What about when they grow taller?" Smudge shivered.

"It's only when the shadows stretch and grow long that I know it's time to fly back to the hive," Bastian said with a grin. "Without them to remind me, I'd probably keep working all night too!"

"That might be hard, since so many flowers close up at night," Jester giggled. "You might get trapped inside one."

"Hard doesn't mean impossible," Bastian shot back.

"You're right, Bastian," Jester admitted, "and Smudge, if you hadn't been kind enough to share your food, I'd still be afraid of your shadow."

"Okay, okay. I get it," Smudge said with another sigh. "Since we need light to help us see, I suppose it means we have to accept the shadows that come along with it."

"Just so!" Bastian exclaimed. "Whenever we see a shadow, a light is shining somewhere."

"Thanks," said Smudge to his friends. "You've helped me understand shadows much better now, and reminded me how important light is—especially sunlight," he added, as he watched the sun disappear from sight, taking with it the day's warmth.

The great ball of light seemed to have been swallowed by the large, grey cloud. Bastian had taken to flying backwards, keeping just far enough ahead of the others so that she could talk to them as they walked, but she shivered as the air turned cooler. Jester scampered along beside Smudge, his small paws going double-time to keep up, and he also seemed to be feeling the cold through his short, tan-coloured fur coat.

"Without the sun we'd freeze and nothing could grow," grunted Barely, ambling along on the other side. He took several more steps before adding, "Not that we'd notice, since we wouldn't be able to see anything."

"Without the sun we'd be too cold, but with it we can be too hot," Smudge mused as he trotted along. "The clouds must be there to make things just right. Hey, Barely, isn't that one of your bear essentials? I'm sure you mentioned it before."

"Yeah. It's not just about hot and cold though—it's about too much or too little of anything. Papa bear used to say it was hard to get anything to *'just right'*, but important to keep trying. He didn't talk much when I was young, but Mama bear made up for it by talking too much. They both practised getting closer to just right and were almost there by the time I was full grown and wandered away. Papa bear had learned to speak up more and

Mama bear had learned to listen." He gave a huge snuffle and wiped a paw across his eyes. "Sorry. I still miss them. I finally realize they were just right for me. I wish I'd told them before leaving. Now it's too late."

"You know what they say," spouted Jester, scampering past Smudge to lay a small paw on Barely's huge one. "Better too late than never."

"Huh?" questioned the baffled bear.

By now they'd reached the bottom of Smudge's driveway and had stopped to say their good-byes. Bastian had once more taken refuge beneath the peak of Barely's right ear, as rain began to patter all around them. The other bees had already left the flowers to head for the hive. At the house there was no sign of Smudge's master.

 # BASHER

"Can we get together again?" Smudge asked his new friends as they made ready to depart.

"Sure, but it will have to be soon if you want me to be awake," Barely replied with his lopsided grin.

"How about in a few days so I can get caught up with my work?" Bastian suggested.

The others nodded in agreement.

"Barely, if you can help guard our hive until winter it would be great. The other bees know you're coming to help, so don't worry if they buzz a bit when they come out to greet you. Just remember to stay still until they recognize you and know you aren't a threat. They'll pay you in honey each day when you're done."

"Sure," Barely said again, licking his lips. "I'll need to spend a few early mornings foraging for other food to make sure I'm ready for my winter nap though. How about you Jester? Are you ready for winter?"

Smudge listened to them talk of how they'd find food to survive over the next several months and felt rather guilty for not having to worry about such things. He was grateful his master had planted so many things throughout their garden. The flowers had helped the bees, which in turn meant Barely would have honey, and Smudge was going to make sure Jester's family had enough seeds and vegetables to last the winter through. Smudge was beginning to understand why some creatures ate others, and, though he felt sorry for the salmon Barely would probably eat, he knew the bear did what he did to stay alive. It was too bad everyone couldn't be friends and find a way to help each other without hurting anyone.

As if in response to his thoughts, Smudge heard Barely say, "I'll try to find as many berries and roots as I can, and if I have to eat salmon, then I'll...I'll..." he paused for a moment, as if trying to figure out how to make it right. His face lit up and he finished by saying, "I'll say sorry to them and try to make sure they don't suffer."

"That's good to hear, Barely—and, Jester, don't you worry about winter, I'll help you get things ready for your family."

The small chipmunk gave an elaborate bow of thanks, then jumped high into the air and did an incredible series of amazing summersaults. He caught hold of a large spray of grass and continued his antics while the others looked on in admiration. They'd not seen him do anything like this before and were quite caught up in the unusual display. In fact, they were so caught up they failed to notice the big dog from next door, crouched down on his belly, slowly creeping toward them.

LESSON B, BE, AND BEE

The shadow from the cloud covered the ground, turning everything to dingy grey, so the big dog cast no shadow to tell them of his approach. Without warning, Smudge found himself picked up by the scruff of the neck and dangling from a powerful set of jaws. He was shaken thoroughly before being roughly tossed up into the air and unexpectedly found himself flying several feet across his front yard. Landing with a painful thump beside the tall fir tree, the little dog gasped for breath. The cushion of needles, which had broken his fall to some extent, poked into his back. He heard Basher give a snarling laugh while horrified cries came from his friends. Jester's small voice could be heard squealing for Barely to run and help. Before Smudge could scramble back to his feet Basher had bounded across the yard and stood over him, teeth barred and snarling in the meanest kind of way. It was too late to try to make himself invisible and Smudge was petrified with fear. His mind was telling him to get up and run away, but none of his muscles would obey.

"Now look here," Barely's reasonable voice came from across the yard and Smudge turned his head in time to see the bear take a few steps forward. All three of his friends were wide-eyed with fear, and for some reason he suddenly felt sorrier for them than for himself. His own fear, however, seemed to lessen.

Basher's eyes were wild with anger, saliva dripped from his open jaws, and, as Barely spoke, the big dog turned toward the group and gave them a doubly furious snarl to warn them away. This stopped Barely in his tracks. The huge bear went quiet and, for a moment, looked the other way. Jester ran to hide behind a rock and stood peering over the edge with terrified eyes. Bastian was buzzing in ever increasing circles, sounding very upset.

Smudge could feel the hot breath of his attacker on his face and closed his eyes so he wouldn't have to witness the big dog's first bite. When it didn't come he opened them again. Basher still stood over him, snarling away. Smudge considered whether to bite one of Basher's legs, but decided it wouldn't be right for him to bite Basher when he didn't want to be bitten himself. Besides, he'd seen dog fights in his life and nobody ever came out looking good.

"If you're going to bite me, just get on with it or go home," he suddenly found himself saying in a defiant voice.

Basher responded by letting go a howl so loud and long that Smudge began to feel frightened again. To his complete surprise, the big dog suddenly leapt into the air, yelping as if he'd been stung by a bee.

"That's it! He's been stung by a bee!" Smudge shouted, scrambling back to his feet and following Basher as he hopped about the yard, favouring one of his back paws.

"Owww! Help me! Owww!" the big dog cried out.

"Why should we help you?" Barely demanded, lumbering over to where the big dog now rolled about on the ground in pain. "You were going to bite our friend."

"I've never bit anyone in my life!" Basher howled.

"Well, that's good to know," Smudge barked in a sharp voice, joining Barely, who was looking down at the suffering dog.

"Please, somebody make the pain stop!" Basher began to whimper pitifully.

"You deserve what you got," growled Barely. "I'm only sorry I didn't give it to you myself."

He looked apologetically at Smudge and the little dog responded with a quick wag of his tail to say Barely was forgiven.

"It's okay," Smudge said to the bear. "You did start to come over, and that counts for something. I know what it's like to be afraid."

"We never know if we'll be brave enough until we're tested," Bastian buzzed in a strained voice. "That's why we shouldn't look down on others when they run away from what's hard for them."

Smudge hadn't seen the tiny bee since Basher had been stung and he breathed a sigh of relief.

"We should help others if there's something they're afraid of and we aren't," squeaked Jester, coming out from behind his rock.

"I was afraid of bees until Smudge helped me," Barely mumbled with head hung low. "Bastian, I'm really sorry I let you down. You shouldn't have had to handle Basher all alone."

The bee nodded wearily as she hovered in the air; somehow she didn't look quite right. Smudge was glad to see her land on the ground and take a well-earned rest from flying.

"Bastian, thanks so much," he began, but a loud whimper brought everyone's attention back to Basher.

"Won't someone have pity on me?" he moaned, holding up his back paw.

No one moved except Jester, who scurried over to the big dog. He looked scared, but carefully stepped over Basher's leg to take a look at his back paw. He began gnawing and tugging at something Smudge couldn't see. The small chipmunk stopped a few times to wipe his face and look nervously up at the big dog's teeth, but Basher only whined encouragingly for him to keep going. With a sudden wave of his small paw, Jester held up what had made the big dog moan so loudly—Bastian's stinger.

"Thank you! Thank you!" Basher said to Jester, trying to lick his wound and the little chipmunk all at the same time.

"It was nothing," Jester said with humility, quickly backing out of the way of the big dog's tongue.

"Can you grow another one, Bastian?" Smudge called out hopefully to the bee. He was trying not to think about what Barely had told him when they'd first met.

"No," she answered from where she rested on the ground. "It's no matter, Smudge. I'm glad I was able to rescue you."

"You're so brave," Smudge said with admiration. "I'm glad to have you as my friend."

"You were brave too," she said softly. "You stood up to Basher in the end."

Smudge held his head up, feeling very pleased by her words. "Jester was brave too," he pointed out, wanting to share the praise.

"Yeah, he went to help Basher, although Basher sure didn't deserve it!" Barely growled, glaring at the big dog.

Basher had been licking his wound, but stopped and climbed to his feet.

"I just wanted someone to see me," he whined wretchedly. "It hurts when no one wants to be your friend."

"Seeing is more important than being seen," grunted Barely, then sat back on his haunches, as if surprised by the smart thing he'd said.

"Oh...okay," Basher replied doubtfully, but seeming ready to listen.

"You have to see what's good in others if you want to have real friends," explained Jester from behind Barely's front paw, where he'd moved to avoid getting another licking. "Snarling may make others look at you, but it sure doesn't make them want to stay and talk."

"I know. I just got tired of trying to make others like me, and then I got mad," Basher admitted.

"At everyone?" Barely enquired in disbelief.

Basher lowered his nose to bat away a cone that had just fallen from the fir tree, barely missing Smudge's head. "I guess it made me feel important too," Basher mumbled.

"You are important," Jester piped up, stepping away from Barely and moving toward the big dog. "You just need friends to show you how."

Basher made a sniffing motion toward Jester, as if that would help him understand what the small creature was saying. "It makes sense the way you put it," he said to the chipmunk. "You're very smart...and brave."

It was Jester's turn to hold his small head up, looking every inch as proud as he should have.

"Understanding the lessons...that's what it's all about," whispered Bastian, from where she lay.

"What lessons?" Basher asked in confusion.

"Don't worry. We'll tell you all about them sometime," Barely grudgingly told the big dog.

"But we have to look after Bastian first," Smudge explained, moving closer to where she lay.

The others crowded around and stood looking at her—even Basher joined them.

"You've helped me a great deal, Smudge," Bastian said, smiling up at him. "I've learned more from you than anyone else I've ever met, and all because you chose not to run away from me yesterday."

"You've taught me loads of things too, Bastian! I can't wait for you to feel better so we can..." Smudge paused, realizing there really was something wrong.

"I'm afraid you won't be able...to teach me much more,"

Bastian tried to reply, but had to stop and cough in between her words.

Barely bent his large snout down toward her, but this time she made no effort to land on it. "I think..." he said, then looked toward Smudge and took a deep breath, "...she's dying."

"What!?" Smudge cried in alarm.

"It's true," Bastian gently told him. "I've lost more than my stinger, I'm afraid."

Smudge looked closely and noticed a part of her back end was definitely missing—that's why she'd looked so odd when she'd reappeared after stinging Basher. Tears welled up in Smudge's eyes.

"Don't cry, Smudge. You neither, Barely," Bastian managed to tease in between gasps for air, "or I'll drown instead of just fading peacefully away...Jester, you'll have to take good care of these two for me."

"I will, Bastian," Jester said proudly, standing at attention with his tail held high in salute.

"And you too, Basher. I bet there's loads of stuff you could...teach these friends of mine."

"Me? Teach something?" Basher sounded astonished, both at being included and at the suggestion he might have something worthwhile to share.

"Sure," Bastian managed to say, "and remember...learning new things is only worthwhile...if you use what you've learned to help yourself and others grow...into something better."

"Oh. Okay. Umm...I'm really sorry what I did made you get hurt," the big dog muttered in a rusty sounding voice, as if unused to saying such things.

"Forgiven," Bastian murmured in reply.

Basher sat down, looking very relieved.

Bastian was obviously getting weaker, and Smudge suddenly found himself feeling more afraid than when Basher had stood snarling over him. He'd just found this great new friend and wasn't ready to lose her.

"I guess...I'll never be able to find out about...that book now. The one with...all the answers," she said in the smallest whisper.

"I'll find out for both of us, Bastian," Smudge promised, "and I'll share whatever I learn with others so we can all know more!"

The bee rolled her eyes, looking up at the sky, but managed a nod of thanks and a last, ghostly smile before resting her head on the earth and closing her eyes.

"No! Wait! Please don't go! You haven't told us the last B lesson yet!" Smudge pleaded, trying to keep his tiny friend from slipping away.

She struggled to open her eyes again, and looked for a long moment at each of them, coming to Smudge last of all.

"*Be...not...afraid,*" the last phrase slipped softly from her mouth and she closed her eyes for the last time.

"Bastian?" Smudge pushed at the bee's body with his nose, but to no avail. Tears flowed freely down his face as he realized she was gone. Yesterday morning she had been just another bothersome bee, and yet in a short time she'd become a dear friend.

"Bastian said not to cry, Smudge," Jester reminded him, stretching to pat the dog on the head, while small tears fell from his own eyes, "and at least we know she wasn't afraid in the end."

"How do we know that?" Barely asked doubtfully, shuffling from foot to foot while he tried to hide loud snuffles behind his huge paws.

"She said it herself: 'Bee not afraid'," Jester replied, wiping away his tears. "Bastian wasn't afraid to die for a friend."

"Umm...I don't think that's what she meant," Smudge said, giving a great sniff. "I think she was giving us the last B lesson."

"Can you explain it to us?" Barely asked anxiously.

Smudge looked up at the sky, which had been washed back to a beautiful shade of blue. All sign of rain had disappeared and the dark cloud had finally passed over the face of the sun. "I think it means don't be afraid to turn and face whatever makes us want to run away. If we can at least be brave enough to do that, and if we do it often enough, we might even forget to be afraid, especially when we're trying to help others."

"You mean like Jester pulling the stinger from Basher's paw, even though he could've gotten bit?" Barely asked hesitantly.

Smudge nodded, lowering his head and rubbing his eyes with both front paws.

"But I wouldn't have hurt him for helping me! I wouldn't hurt anybody!" Basher protested.

"You hurt Smudge," Jester pointed out.

"And it sounds like you've hurt plenty of others with your snarls and growls," Barely added.

Smudge almost smiled, despite feeling so sad. It was plain that Barely didn't realize just how much his own growls could sound like those of the big dog.

"But we're very glad to hear you won't be doing anymore of that," Smudge said seriously to Basher, "and if you think having friends is worth the hard work, you might want to try getting to know us better." He turned to Jester, looking quite stern. "As for you, I want your promise to be more careful after this. You and

Bastian have shown us what real courage is, but it seems Barely and I will have to teach you more common sense. You have a family to think of and can't go taking any more chances like that."

"Yeah. From now on Smudge and I will take care of things and you just stay hidden behind a rock until we tell you it's safe," Barely rumbled. "That is, at least until your family's grown."

"But you're both part of my family now," Jester chattered with a watery smile. "In my clan, family means anyone who's willing to help."

Barely raised a huge paw and gently patted first Jester then Smudge on the top of their much smaller heads. "In my cave, that makes you honorary bears," he said.

The chipmunk bobbed his head in thanks, looking quite proud of the honour the bear was bestowing on them. Smudge wagged his tail vigorously, saying, "You're both my family and my friends now. I'll have to wait a while before inviting you over to my house, though. I don't think my master's quite up to that yet." He gave a rueful grin, then glanced down at the ground and the smile left his face. He was going to miss Bastian terribly. With a heavy sigh of sadness he bent his head and, using his teeth, gently picked her up by one fragile wing. He carefully carried her back to the flower garden where she'd spent so much of her life. Digging a small hole, Smudge carefully laid his tiny bee friend down and covered her with a blanket of soft earth.

Jester scurried to the prettiest flower he could find and gnawed through the stem. He then brought back the sweet-smelling petals and laid them over the brown mound in a gesture of farewell.

Barely ambled over to stand with them and Basher followed, still limping on his sore paw. The friends stood quietly together for a few minutes, and then Barely cleared his throat, which seemed to have tightened up.

"Bastian, you were the wisest creature I've ever met," he stated with a muffled sniff.

"You were braver than anyone I've ever known," Jester chattered in a shrill voice.

"And were the most humble bee," Smudge softly added.

"And the most willing to help your friends," came a tiny voice from above.

"And the hardest worker of all," buzzed another tiny voice.

"And the one most willing to try and understand every bee's perspective," hummed a third.

The friends looked up to see a crowd of bees droning above their heads. They were flying in a slow, solemn dance that was beautiful to watch. The pace quickened, and soon they looked like one swirling ball of yellow and black. Suddenly they broke apart and moved into new positions, hovering together in a sort of bee rainbow that spelled out three short words:

Smudge said them aloud: "Woe. Bee. Gone."

The late afternoon sun caught his eye through the arc of bees and, for a moment, he was sure he saw Bastian busy at work on a beautiful white flower with a golden centre.

It glowed faintly with a strange, soft light and hung suspended in the sky just below where Bastian's fellow bees had gathered. Its petals held a few brilliant drops of rain, and they sparkled richly in the sun, whose bright rays streamed down along Bastian's tiny body and delicate, flashing wings. Somehow, in the warm bath of light, she looked different than Smudge remembered her—softer somehow with thicker bands of rich black and yellow colouring around the middle, yet still the same bee. He realized his eyes were seeing differently now and was amazed as he finally understood he was seeing the bee in full colour. Pausing from her work, Bastian looked up and gave Smudge her best, beaming smile. Smudge smiled back, wagging his tail as hard as he could.

A loud voice suddenly broke the silence of the moment. "Smudge? Here boy. Where's that dratted dog got to?"

At the sound of his master's voice, the vision of the flower and bee faded from the little dog's sight.

"It's time for me to say good-bye," Smudge told his friends.

Jester and Barely briefly touched noses, and then did the same with Smudge as a gesture of continuing friendship. Smudge turned to look at Basher, who hesitated for a moment before he too came and touched his nose to that of the little dog.

"Sorry," Basher muttered.

"It's okay," Smudge murmured in reply.

"Oh my gosh!" the loud voice hollered again. "A bear! Smudge! Look out! Run!"

Hearing the yelling and catching the scent of a human, which he'd been taught to be wary of when still a cub, Barely grunted a quick, "Good-bye and see you soon," to the trio. Then he turned and raced at an incredible speed back up over the mountain and out of sight.

"Wow! I never knew he could run that fast!" Smudge said, a bit startled.

"Oh sure. Bears can really move when they have to," Basher replied knowledgeably. "Don't get the wrong idea about others. Just because they seem a little slow to you, it doesn't mean they are."

"I hear you," replied Smudge, thinking of the turtle in the fairy-tale.

They watched as Smudge's master peered nervously out from behind one of the pillars at the front of the house.

"My human likes to say: 'if you don't want to slip, don't run on ice'," Basher sighed.

"Mine says that too," Smudge replied.

"Really? Sometimes it feels like I'm always running on ice," Basher continued. "I just can't seem to stop myself."

"Perhaps we can help you," chattered Jester, moving closer to the big dog.

Basher threw Jester a big grin and wagged his tail, sweeping away several leaves as he did so.

"Hey, that would be great. Thanks again for helping me, by the way, and I'm really very sorry about your friend." Jester nodded, looking nervously toward where the human stood frantically waving his arms at Smudge.

"You'd better get going," Smudge told them.

Needing no further encouragement, Jester whispered a hurried, "Good-bye," made a dash for the nearest rock, and disappeared from sight. Basher paused a moment longer to invite Smudge to his house for a visit the following day. Smudge was still feeling a bit uncertain about Basher after everything that had happened, but decided to give him a chance to prove himself.

"Alright," he said, accepting the offer.

Basher seemed quite pleased, and with another quick wag of his tail he, too, was gone.

Smudge turned to his master, who had calmed down a little after seeing Barely make a bee-line for the forest. The scare had got him pretty upset, however, and he continued to shout at Smudge without once considering the neighbours.

"Smudge, are you deaf? Get over here now! You need to learn when to run away and when to just sit there wagging your silly tail!"

A bee whizzed by Smudge, and then another and another as Bastian's bee friends began buzzing about the human to let him know they weren't happy with his hollering at Smudge. Any friend of Bastian's was also a friend of theirs.

"Oh bother, now where have all these dratted bees come from? I'll go fetch the bottle of Bee-Be-Gone," the human said and stomped off into the house.

Smudge didn't want to see the bees get hurt trying to protect him and so began explaining. "It's okay. He saw the bear and was afraid for me, that's all. That's how humans act when they think their family is in trouble."

The bees buzzed about his head, talking over what Smudge had said, but none seemed in a hurry to leave. Smudge began to worry more.

"Hey, you have to buzz off now! My master's gone to get something that could hurt you. I don't want anyone from Bastian's family to get hurt."

Hearing his fear-filled statement, the bees buzzed loudly in alarm and flew off in every direction at once. Smudge was alone once more.

A DIFFERENT PERSPECTIVE

Smudge sat quietly for awhile, thinking of everything that had happened. He raised a paw to scratch an itch behind his ear, but paused mid-scratch. A new thought had occurred to him. The fact was, he hadn't expected to learn anything special from all the creatures who'd come wandering into his yard over the last few days. Though he'd first mistaken Bastian for a dangerous creature, Barely for a slow-moving monster, and Jester for a horrible pest, he'd soon found out how wrong he'd been. None of them had turned out to be what he'd expected, not even that mean old bully, Basher. In the end, by getting to know these others, who were all so very different from him, he'd learned more about himself.

"Bastian would probably have said the best way to see ourselves is through another's eyes," Smudge chuckled under his breath.

He began to make his way back to the front porch, but as he did he heard a soft rustle. A long snake slithered from under a nearby bush, tongue darting in and out like it was tasting the air. It slid along the edge of the pavement, gliding into holes in the cement and then out again as if looking for something in those small crevasses. It spotted the dog and came to an abrupt stop.

"Sssstay away from me or I'll sssstrike you," it warned with a hiss.

Smudge almost turned to run, but stopped. Taking a deep breath, he forced himself to look straight into the cold, slitted eyes of the snake. Now he understood what was meant about eyes being both windows and mirrors. Smudge was not surprised to see the fear those snake eyes reflected back at him. Suddenly Bastian's words were ringing in his head.

"Be not afraid," Smudge found himself saying aloud.

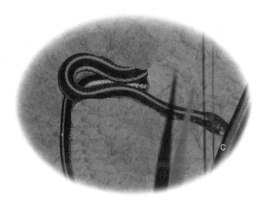

Hearing these words the snake seemed to relax a bit. "What doessss that mean?" it demanded.

Smudge struggled to explain it. "I guess it means we should try to get to know and understand one another so we won't be afraid of each other."

"I ssssee. Sssso why should it matter if we're afraid?" the snake asked.

Smudge hadn't expected such a question. Too him it mattered very much that he overcome his fears. It hadn't occurred to him that others might see no purpose in doing so. "Well, if we're afraid of each other we can't become friends," he explained further.

"Why would we want to be friendssss?" questioned the snake in a cold voice.

The dog was almost at a loss for words. He tried hard to think of a good answer, but thinking fast had never been his strong point. Then he remembered how happy Bastian had been, buzzing in circles above the heads of her new-found friends as she shared her lessons.

"The reason we'd want to be friends is so we can learn from each other," Smudge replied, adding, "and then we wouldn't want to eat each other for supper."

"I like my ssssupper," the snake hissed.

"Well, what about the frogs? How do you think they feel about being eaten?" demanded Smudge.

"Frogssss are there for a purpossssse—my ssssupper. Why should I care how they feel?" the snake responded with a smile, though one that didn't reach its venomous eyes.

"Well, what if another creature was about to step on you?" Smudge tried again. "Wouldn't you want them to care about how you felt?"

"I'd sssstrike them firssst!" the snake hissed in anger.

Smudge shook his head, almost ready to give up, but decided to give it one more try.

"Look, snake, if you don't want to care about others, that's up to you, but in the end you'll have no friends and you'll be all alone. What if all the other creatures in the world ended up making friends except for the snakes? We'd all be together talking and laughing and sharing food and you wouldn't be there. Is that what you want?"

"I don't want that, no," said the snake, "but I prefer my ssssupper."

"Well, I prefer my friends. Do you have any friends?" Smudge asked.

The serpent seemed taken aback by the question. Smudge couldn't help noticing how it hesitated before answering.

"I don't need friendssss. I take what I need when I need it. If we were friendssss I'd have to be niccccce to you. What if I got hungry and there wassss nothing to eat but you, and you were my friend?"

"Why I guess we'd just have to starve together!" Smudge laughed. "That's what friends do for each other."

"They sssstarve together?" The snake seemed baffled by this idea.

"They do whatever they need to do to help each other," explained Smudge. "That way, no matter how tough things get, they don't have to face it alone. I'll tell you what. You seem like a nice enough snake, and a pretty smart one too."

The snake's forked tongue slipped in and out a few times at this unexpected compliment.

"So, if you ever change your mind," Smudge continued, "and want to spend some time together learning new things, just come by and let me know. I'd be happy to sit and talk with you. I know several other friends who just might be willing to do the same. You'd be surprised by all the things you can learn, and we'd probably learn things from you too!"

"You would?" asked the snake, seeming suspicious. "Well, perhapsssss I'll think about it."

It stared back at Smudge for a moment longer, then turned its body as if to leave. Suddenly it spun back around, raised itself up high and hissed venomously, as if expecting Smudge to run away. Smudge didn't move from where he stood, feeling afraid for himself, but also very sad for the snake. He realized it wasn't ready to want to understand yet.

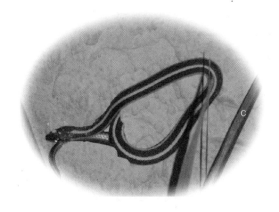

Smudge hoped that by staying still, the snake would see that it was itself, not Smudge, who was choosing to move away from this chance for greater understanding.

Seeing no threat to itself in Smudge's steady stance, the snake stopped its hissing and dropped back onto the pavement. It gave a barely visible nod of its head in Smudge's direction, and he saw reluctant respect gleam from its slitted eyes. Then the serpent turned its long body and slithered silently away.

With head held high, Smudge walked fearlessly toward the porch of his house. The front door banged open and his master reappeared, frantically spraying liquid from a can at any and all winged creatures unlucky enough to fly by. Coughs and splutters were heard from tiny, flying bugs as they gasped for clean air and sped away in all directions from the monstrous human with the spray can. Shaking his head, Smudge sighed and began to consider how he could help his master look at other creatures from a different perspective...or two.

The End

About this project

These stories were written with the intention that all net proceeds be given to charitable and/or non-profit organizations. All those who have participated in this book's making and distribution (excluding printer and shipping and handling agents) have freely donated their time and talents. A list of individuals, businesses, non-profit organizations and charitable organizations who are lawfully selling these books and donating the net proceeds to a non-profit or charitable organization will be listed on our web site: www.writedimensions.ca.

How you can become a part of this charitable book project

1. Visit our web site and complete our order form (this will be sent directly to the printer).

2. You will be charged for printing, shipping and delivery to your location. Allow several weeks for printing and delivery.

3. You are entitled to recover your printing, shipping and delivery costs from the proceeds of the book sales.

4. All net proceeds (after recovering your costs) must be donated to a charity or non-profit organization of your choice. If you are a charity or non-profit organization who is participating in this project, you may retain the net proceeds for your organization.

5. Your name, business name, charity or non-profit organization name will be published on the Write Dimensions web site along with your contact information and the name of the charity or non-profit organization which you choose to support.

6. Restrictions may apply. The author reserves the right to cancel or revise the terms of this charitable project and to ensure that the terms and conditions of this project are being met by all involved.

Check your government web site for more information on charitable gift-giving.

To find out where to purchase an individual copy of this book, see the list of distributors at www.writedimensions.wordpress.com